CalFire book 1

Controlled Burn

Sherryl D. Hancock

PRESS

Published by Vulpine Press in the United Kingdom in 2021

ISBN: 978-1-83919-162-6

www.vulpine-press.com

Author's note

In 1905 the Board of Forestry was established, as was the position of the State Forester. This was the beginning of the California Department of Forestry and Fire Protection, otherwise known as Cal Fire. The men and women of Cal Fire are dedicated to the fire protection and stewardship of over 31 million acres of California's privately owned wildlands. In addition, the department provides varied emergency services in 36 of the State's 58 counties via contracts with local governments.

It's a tumultuous time in California where there really is no fire season anymore, since forest and wildland fires start at all times of the year, and often rage for weeks or months. In 2020 not only was there a health pandemic, but there was also a record fire season, over 4.2 million acres of land was burned in California. Wade Crowfoot, the head of the Natural Resources is quoted as saying, "We're seeing impacts today that we thought we'd see by midcentury." It doesn't bode well for the direction of California's wildlands.

This series is dedicated in its entirety to the brave men and women of Cal Fire, and all firefighters statewide who put their lives on the line to protect the natural beauty of the great state of California. Thank you for your service!

Photo taken by Alićia Rutter and Bryon Hawkins from the Tubbs Fire, October 8–31, 2017. It burned 39,807 acres and destroyed 5643 structures, killing 22 people. Bryon's home is the one burned down in this photo. Alićia is Sherryl D. Hancock's niece.

Acknowledgements

Thank you to Sarah Markel who was kind enough to share her firefighting experience and expertise with me.

Controlled Burn

Prologue

"I'm sorry, babe, I don't know if I can do this anymore…" Hunter Briggs said out loud, even though she was the only one in the room.

Tears streamed from her eyes as she lay with her head on her wife Heather's pillow. It was morning, but still dark outside. It was the day after Christmas, a holiday Heather had sincerely loved, and had endeavored to make great for everyone around her. It had also been the first Christmas without her and it had been brutal. It was made worse by a wedding Hunter had been invited to, where the happy couple was very much in love and it had only raked Hunter's heart over the coals seeing it.

She'd managed to drink herself into a stupor, ending with a long walk along the cliffs of Mendocino, part of her hoping that the highly unstable cliffs would just give way and she'd fall to her death. Or that she'd freeze to death with the icy cold wind coming in off the ocean. They were morose thoughts, she knew, but they were there all the same. When neither of those things had happened, she'd taken a cab back to the house she had shared with her wife of sixteen years and dropped into their bed, hoping to pass out. That hadn't happened either.

Instead she'd lain in their bed, alternately staring at the ceiling and all the things in the room that Heather had bought or made to make their home theirs to its very core. Everything in the two-story, wood construction house emanated Heather. The property boasted an art studio, home gym, and green house as well as a helicopter pad on its grounds. Every inch of the house had Heather's touch on it, her colors and her style, mixed with Hunter's. Heather's style usually won out, however, in ways such as the many butterflies around the house in paintings, sculptures, and even stained-glass panels. Heather had loved all things butterfly, her favorite being the orange and black monarch. She'd been deeply concerned with the decline of the monarchs and had been heavily involved in a local group trying to save them. It had been one of the many things Heather had been involved in.

As the morning dawned, Hunter found herself staring at the delicate glass butterfly hanging down from the ceiling fan. It was the last one Heather had bought on their final trip out of the house, when Heather had started to become restless. Memories of that cold but sunny day crowded Hunter's mind, making her ache all over again. She remembered Heather's smile when she'd found the beautiful delicate butterfly figurine in one of the local stores in Fort Bragg. Hunter was convinced the shopkeeper, Annie, had purposely ordered it for Heather. Everyone had known Heather was dying, and it was breaking everyone's hearts. Worse still, everyone who'd known Hunter her entire life knew it was killing Hunter at the same time.

In the eleven months since Heather's passing, everyone had been supportive and there for her at every turn. It made Hunter even more dedicated to her town, not that she hadn't devoted her life to her home and the forests that surrounded it by being a firefighter for Cal Fire. She'd risked her life time and time again to save people and property in Mendocino County.

As Hunter stared at the glass butterfly, twisting slowly in the light breeze coming through the open windows, she felt tears back up on her again.

"I know I said I'd get on with my life..." she said, her voice halting, "but God babe I miss you so much...Sam's gonna be headed off to college in the summer...and then it'll just be me again...I don't know if I can do this..." She shook her head as tears slid from her eyes in a steady stream again.

A flutter of color caught her attention then, and her eyes widened as she realized that it was one of the lovely black and orange winged insects that Heather had loved so much, that had just made its way into the house via the open window. Hunter moved to sit up in her complete shock.

"Shouldn't you have headed south by now?" Hunter asked the surprising little visitor. She watched it flutter its way over to a picture of Heather and Hunter on their wedding day where it hovered for a moment.

As Hunter continued to watch, the butterfly, resplendent in its stained-glass window-like wings, flew to the picture of Heather that Hunter had on her nightstand. It was a picture that Hunter loved of Heather, because it was how she'd always seen her wife. In the picture Heather was turned at an angle, her blue eyes looking down. Her long blonde hair was swept to the side and woven into a loose fishtail-style braid with tendrils escaping to frame her face.

The butterfly landed on the picture, its antennae waving in Hunter's direction. Hunter turned her head slightly, canting it as the strangest sensation crawled up her spine.

"Babe?" Hunter breathed, not daring to hope, but wanting it to be true so badly it physically hurt.

To Hunter's amazement the butterfly slowly flapped its wings then alighted, fluttering toward Hunter, hovering in front of her for a long moment, almost like it was staring at her.

"Whoa…" Hunter breathed, as the butterfly moved to land on the nightstand, on top of Hunter's phone. Hunter wasn't sure what was happening, but it was definitely odd, and the sensation that she somehow *knew* this delicate little visitor just wouldn't go away.

The butterfly sat on the device's screen for a full minute, and Hunter kept getting the nagging feeling that she was supposed to be understanding something. The hair on the back of her neck was standing up. An incoming email lit up the screen beneath the butterfly. Hunter grinned as the winged creature practically hopped off the phone.

"Scare you, itty bitty?" she asked as she reached for the device.

She opened the email she'd just received and started to chuckle. She glanced around looking for the butterfly and to her shock found that it was hovering just over her right shoulder, just like Heather had always done when she'd stand behind Hunter as she'd be reading something.

"You have to be kidding me, right?" Hunter said to the butterfly, as if she were talking to Heather herself. "Is this a hint,

4

babe?" she asked holding up the phone, as if she would actually get an answer.

The butterfly alighted on her shoulder for a long moment and Hunter debated with herself about the odds of this tiny creature being her deceased wife. Was it possible? Hunter had always been skeptical of the supernatural, but the way the butterfly was acting, was just beyond coincidental, wasn't it? Was she just losing her mind now? But as her little visitor continued to sit on her shoulder, wings flapping slowly up and down, Hunter suddenly just knew beyond a shadow of a doubt that Heather had indeed come to her when she needed her most. She felt both elated and sad at the same time.

"Okay, honey, okay, I got the message…" Hunter said, smiling as the butterfly fluttered up again moving back toward the window.

Just then, there was a knock on the door and a voice called, "Mom?"

Hunter glanced toward the window and saw that the butterfly had stopped and was hovering near it.

"Gotta check on her too, huh?" Hunter asked softly toward the butterfly, even as she turned to answer her daughter's query. "Yeah babe? Come on in," she said as she reached up to wipe away tears.

Samantha Briggs, the spitting image of her mother, opened the door and caught the movement Hunter had made to attempt to hide her wet cheeks.

"Who were you talking—oh!" she exclaimed as she saw the butterfly. "Hello," she said to the insect, her smile soft. She looked so much like Heather at that moment, Hunter felt her throat constrict again.

The butterfly made its exit then, and Hunter closed her eyes feeling tears slip down her cheeks again. Suddenly Samantha was there, hugging her. Hunter held onto Samantha, doing her best to control her tears, knowing that she was supposed to be the strong one right now, not their seventeen-year-old daughter.

"I miss her too," Samantha said against Hunter's shoulder.

"I think that was her," Hunter said.

Samantha pulled back, looking up at Hunter. "You do?" she asked hopefully.

It warmed Hunter's heart that Samantha didn't look at her like she was crazy, and that she'd believe it if Hunter told her it was true.

"Well, it's December," Hunter said, "and from everything your mom told me about them, they have usually gone south by now. She hovered in front of our wedding picture, and landed on this one, and my phone, just before it lit up with a message. Then when I was reading the email, guess where she was…"

Samantha's smile was wide. "Right there," she said, reaching up to touch the back of Hunter's right shoulder.

"Yep," Hunter said nodding.

"Oh my God, that was her…" Samantha said her eyes shining.

"I hit a rough patch last night and this morning," Hunter said, always honest with Samantha, "and I think she was here to tell me to knock it the hell off."

Samantha laughed softly, then bit her lip.

"I guess she's trying to tell you to get on with it, huh?"

"Oh you have no idea," Hunter said, rolling her eyes and shaking her head as she handed Samantha her phone. The email she'd received was still up on the screen.

Hunter got off the bed as Samantha settled against the headboard, reading the message. Hunter walked into the bathroom and ran water to wash her face.

"Who's Koriander Stanton?" Samantha called.

Hunter grinned, looking at herself in the mirror. "Someone I used to know."

Chapter 1

Koriander "Kori" Stanton stepped off the bus that had brought her to the Fort Bragg California Department of Forestry offices for check-in to her first post. Looking around, she was amazed by all the activity. She also couldn't believe she was finally here! She'd completed her six-week firefighter academy in Ione, California and had been thrilled to receive an assignment to Fort Bragg. It had been a shock to her system, traveling from Southern California where she lived, to the Northern California coast, but she'd marveled at the beautiful northern coastline for the entire trip. It was late fall, and she'd been warned that it got very cold in Fort Bragg and that she'd better pack warm clothes. Having grown up in Los Angeles, Kori had never really dealt with cold weather; it was almost always sunny and seventy degrees in Southern California.

As she was hustled into the office to do her check-in, she did her best to take everything in, not wanting to miss a moment of this. It had been her dream to fight fires. She had seen so many reports on TV about the fires in Southern California that had taken lives and destroyed properties. She'd also seen the brave firefighters putting themselves between the people and their homes, and Kori had known then that it was what she'd wanted to do. On career day in high school, The California Department of Forestry had a booth and had given her information about becoming a firefighter. She'd seen their uniforms and gear and had taken in the way that they carried themselves, and she'd known then that she had to work for them. It took another two years to get her application accepted by CDF, but she'd gotten her job offer and had accepted it happily even though it was five hundred and fifty miles north of where she lived

"Might want to watch your six," said a voice from behind her.

Kori jumped, turning around. She found herself staring up into eyes that were as close to silver as she'd ever seen. Those light-colored eyes were glittering with amusement as they stared down at her.

"You must be the new girl," the woman with nice eyes said. Her voice was rich and held a hint of humor.

Kori found that she couldn't formulate a reply as the woman smiled at her. She couldn't reply because she suddenly couldn't think past that brilliant smile or the sparkling silver eyes. Instead, she nodded mutely. The woman's lips pressed together and curled into a grin, as if she knew she'd just completely undone her some-how.

"You'll need a ride to the camp," the woman said, her eyes still dancing with amusement. "I'm headed back that way if you don't want to climb back onto that smelly bus with all those guys."

"I, um, yeah, that would be great," Kori said, finally regaining her faculties.

"Cool," the woman said, grinning. She put her hand out to Kori. "I'm Hunter."

"Koriander," Kori said, taking Hunter's hand and shaking it, even as Hunter canted her head at her.

"People actually call you that?" Hunter asked, her tone playful.

Kori laughed softly. "Not really, no, except my parents."

"So I can get away with calling you Kori, right?" Hunter asked, a smile on her lips.

"Yes, yes you can," Kori said, feeling like she was making a fool out of herself at this point.

"Okay, I'm the black El Camino out in the yard, just come find me when you get done in here," Hunter said, nodding toward the desk where everyone was checking in.

An hour later, Kori was in the passenger seat of a classic El Camino and doing her best not to completely freak out every time Hunter went flying around a sharp curve.

"I take it you drive these roads a lot?" Kori said as she put her hand out to grip the dashboard.

"Babe, I learned to drive on these roads," Hunter said, her eyes sparkling with a challenge. "Am I totally freaking you out?"

"Um, no…" Kori said, her tone far from convincing.

Hunter laughed. "Yeah, I believe that one."

They were both silent for a few minutes. Kori looked over at Hunter, taking in the way she sat, looking very comfortable behind the wheel of the classic car. She had shaggy black hair, and a lean build as well as a lean face with a strong jawline. She didn't appear to wear even a speck of makeup. She looked like a tomboy with her jeans, Converse tennis shoes, and dark flannel shirt.

"So where are you from?" Hunter asked after a long silence.

"Los Angeles," Kori said, smiling.

"Wow, way down there?" Hunter asked. "Why the hell did ya come up here?"

Kori shrugged. "It was my first job offer, it took me two years to get in. I didn't want to give up any chance, and I'm just waiting for LA, you know?"

Hunter nodded. "I guess I got lucky on my first pass," she said, grinning.

"So you grew up here?" Kori asked, assuming that had been what she meant by learning to drive on 'these' roads.

"Yep," Hunter said, grinning. "Born and raised, with a short military intermission."

"You were in the military?" Kori asked.

"Yep, joined the army long enough to learn to fly helicopters and rack up enough hours to get my license when I got out," Hunter said, waggling her eyebrows.

"So you fly helicopters?" Kori asked, impressed.

"I can," Hunter said, "but so far CDF isn't seeing fit to let me fly for them, so I'm biding my time."

Kori nodded. "It's still a boys club, huh?"

"Totally!" Hunter said, rolling her eyes.

"So what's the camp like?"

"Well, you'll be the only other woman there, so…" Hunter said, letting her voice trail off.

"Do we have to bunk with them too?" Kori asked, making a face.

"Well, see, that's where you're helpin' me out," Hunter said, grinning. "Since there's now two of us, they saw fit to give us our own little space, which, thank you, thank you, thank you, isn't great, but it's better than having to listen to men fart and snore all night."

"I'm glad I could help you out," Kori said, grinning.

"Trust me, you don't want to be stuck in a room full of men after pizza and beer night." Hunter laughed.

"Oh I believe you," Kori said, nodding. "There were three of us girls at the academy, and thankfully they decided we were safer by ourselves too."

"Comes in handy being a girl sometimes, huh?" Hunter said, her tone sly.

"Big time!" Kori agreed.

Kori noticed the music that Hunter had on in the car was rock. She was playing older bands like Boston, Black Sabbath, The Eagles, with some newer stuff like Def Leppard and Van Halen.

"So a rocker girl, huh?" Kori commented.

"All the way! Let me guess," she said, canting her head to the side, her look appraising, "you're a Cyndi Lauper kinda girl, right?"

Kori opened her mouth in shock, then closed it nodding, looking slightly embarrassed.

Hunter chuckled, shaking her head. "I knew it. I'll try not to hold that against you."

A little while later they pulled into the camp. Hunter showed her where the Squad Boss's office was so she could check in.

"I'll take your gear to our bunk house," Hunter said as she pulled the cover up on the El Camino's bed.

"Thanks," Kori said, smiling, and then turned to walk toward the office Hunter had directed her to.

Hunter leaned against the back of the El Camino watching Kori walk away and biting her lip. Damn the girl was hot! With long, wavy blonde hair, green eyes, and a perfect little figure, Kori was a stunner that was for damned sure. Hunter wasn't at all sure the girl could fight fire worth a damn, but she was an awfully nice addition to the scenery around the camp.

Three weeks later, she found that while Kori did her very best, the girl was still very green when it came to firefighting. They were doing a lot of training and prepping before winter set in and Kori was struggling to keep up. A number of the guys started calling her a 'dolly' because she was 'cute but useless'. Hunter heard it and had a few choice words for them. One particular evening she overheard two of the guys talking about Kori in a derogatory way.

"Hodge, I remember when you almost set your own ass on fire trying to do a controlled burn, and Franklin, you've seriously forgotten that little mishap with the hose and the boss's truck?" Hunter drawled as she leaned against the side of the mess hall, her legs crossed casually at the ankles, her arms folded over her chest. "She's new," Hunter said, her tone succinct, "and you need to lay off her and let her find her feet."

"Man, Briggs, you got it bad or what?" Hodge said, never one to handle criticism well.

"Got what bad, Briggs?" Hunter asked, coming off the building her demeanor no longer casual. "You think I'm like you? And judge women only by how fuckable they are? See? That's the difference between me and you," she said, her tone snide. "I like what's in their head, not just whether or not they'll give me head."

She stepped closer to Hodge, her look threatening. "Lay off Kori, or I'll fuckin' make ya, you got it?"

"What do you think you can do, Briggs?" Hodge said, his tone all bravado.

Silver eyes flared and turned impossibly lighter as Hunter growled out the words, "You want to find out?"

Something in the look in Hunter's eyes warned Franklin, even if Hodge was still too full of himself to catch it. Franklin grabbed Hodge's arm in an attempt to pull his friend away. But Hodge refused to budge.

"You don't scare me, Briggs," Hodge sneered.

"You might want to step off right about now…" Hunter said, narrowing her eyes.

"I don't think I will," Hodge said, pushing his chest out.

"Throw or go home, Hodge," Hunter challenged.

Without a word, Hodge threw a punch at Hunter's midsection. She surprised him by bringing her arm up and through with enough force to not only block his punch but back hand him in the face. Dropping one leg behind her, she bounced on the balls of her feet, and it was obvious she was ready for a fight; her hands were up in a boxer's stance, her look at Hodge telling him that he'd just messed with the wrong girl.

Everyone at the camp knew Hunter was gay, she'd made it clear enough to all of them right up front. It rankled all of the men that Kori hung out with Hunter more than she hung out with the group. Male egos were so very fragile.

Hodge recovered from his temporary shock and moved in to go after Hunter. She easily sidestepped his attack, kicking him in the ass on the way by, causing him to stumble and fall face first in the dirt. He moved to his feet quickly and charged at Hunter, catching her in the mid-section, trying to knock her down. Hunter spun to her left, breaking his hold on her, and bringing her leg up and around as she did. Hodge wasn't fast enough to see the spin kick she used to knock him out.

"Jesus, Briggs!" Franklin yelled, as he moved to help Hodge.

"He started it," Hunter said, adjusting her shirt, "I just finished it." With that, she walked away.

Kori eased off the side of the building and walked around the other side of the chow hall to keep from being seen. She'd heard the entire conversation, since she'd been leaving the mess hall at the same time Hodge and Franklin had. She'd been about to say something to them when Hunter had spoken up and had hidden behind the building to listen to what was said.

She'd grown to like Hunter more in the last few days. Hunter was patient with her, explaining things when she messed up, rather than just shaking her head and walking away like a lot of the men did. It was very frustrating to have people treat you like you were stupid. She knew it was all part of being new to the field, and being a woman, but she also knew it would be a lot worse if she didn't have Hunter there to help her. For that she was very grateful.

Kori made her way back to their bunk house, walking into the room hesitantly. She saw Hunter lying on her bunk, her head resting on her hands that were up behind her head. Walking over, Kori sat down on the side of the bunk, looking down at Hunter.

"I heard that whole thing," she told her.

Hunter's silver eyes shifted from the ceiling to her, searching, then she shrugged.

"They're just men being men," she said, "don't take it too seriously."

"Should I take the fact that you just got into a fight with a guy because you were defending me seriously?" Kori asked, grinning.

A smile tugged at Hunter's lips. "No, you shouldn't take that too seriously either. Hell, I'm just as bad as they are sometimes."

"What do you mean?" Kori asked, surprised by Hunter's statement.

"I mean, I whore around and use women too, they aren't the only ones that do that kind of thing."

"You whore around?" Kori asked cynically, using Hunter's words.

Hunter grinned. "Tourists, babe, tourists."

"Awww," Kori murmured, nodding her green eyes widening slightly. "Female tourists, right?" she asked, canting her head to the side, already learning that gesture from Hunter.

Hunter looked back at Kori for a long moment, her lips curled in a sardonic grin. "Are you asking me if I'm gay?"

Kori rolled her eyes heavenward, in consideration of her answer, but then she nodded. "I'm just confirming what I already thought."

"I see," Hunter said, her grin still in place, "well, yes, I am."

Kori nodded. She'd already guessed at it, but Kori had wanted to hear it from Hunter.

"So they think you're interested, and that's why you're being nice to me?" Kori asked.

"Basically yeah," Hunter said nodding, "and let's get something straight here. I'm not being nice to you, I'm doing what I consider my job."

16

Kori nodded, understanding what Hunter meant.

"Well, I appreciate it," Kori said.

"Right," Hunter said, "my thinking you're hot is a completely separate thing."

Kori's mouth dropped open and Hunter started to laugh at her expression. Kori wasn't sure if Hunter had meant it or not, but before she could ask someone knocked on the door to their cabin.

"Stanton, you got a phone call!" the man yelled.

"Okay, thanks!" Kori replied, getting up from Hunter's bunk.

"We're not done talking," Kori told Hunter with narrowed eyes.

Hunter simply chuckled. Kori left to go pick up the phone call. It was from her husband, Tom. The conversation was short and stilted; much like all their conversations had been ever since she'd taken this assignment. Walking back to the bunk house, Kori found herself feeling a little depressed. Inside she saw that Hunter was no longer in her bunk, and she heard the shower running.

Hunter emerged from the small bathroom dressed in jeans and a black long-sleeved shirt with a white T-shirt underneath. Her hair was damp from the shower, and Kori noted that she wore cologne, like a man would, but she liked the smell, and thought it fit Hunter pretty well.

"Are you going out?" Kori asked.

"Yeah," Hunter said nodding, "just headed over to Mendo to a couple of bars over there. Do you want to come?"

"Would you mind?" Kori asked, not wanting to intrude.

"Wouldn't mind at all," Hunter said, grinning.

"Cool, let me throw on some makeup and run a brush through my hair," Kori said, smiling as she got up from her bunk.

Twenty minutes later, Hunter was reminded that her roommate was a hot woman. Kori wore jeans and a dark blue sweater that fit her curves nicely. She hadn't gone overboard on the makeup, just using enough to enhance her features. The girl was way sexier than any woman had a right to be as far as Hunter was concerned.

Kori noticed that Hunter now wore black combat boots and a black leather biker jacket. She looked like the consummate 'greaser' from the fifties, but in a sexy way. It surprised Kori how often she thought of Hunter in the same category as men, comparing her to them and thinking that she came out way ahead of them all. She wasn't sure if that was normal or if she was just losing her mind. It wasn't like she hadn't been around anyone who was gay before, she had. Her parents were the original hippies with their free love attitudes and 'tree hugger' ways. Kori knew that her opinions on life had been formed by them and it was because of them that she was open to people being who they were. Even so, she found herself fascinated by Hunter constantly.

That night, driving over the hills that would take them to Highway 1 and then to Mendocino, Kori felt brave enough to start asking some of the questions she'd been thinking about.

"When did you know you were gay?" Kori asked.

Hunter glanced over at her, obviously surprised by the question. Then she shrugged. "I think I always knew, kind of how you probably knew you were attracted to boys. I knew I wasn't, and that girls held all kinds of interest for me."

"Like what?" Kori asked.

Hunter grinned. "Like this girl in my class in fourth grade…she had the longest hair and it was silky and shiny all the time. I found myself just wanting to run my hands through it…" Her voice trailed off with a wistful smile.

"Did you ever do it?" Kori asked, her look expectant.

Hunter laughed. "Nah, I didn't want her to think I was weird or something. She was pretty popular. Years later, though…that's a different story…" she said, grinning roguishly.

"Years later…what happened?" Kori asked, finding herself feeling a bit too anticipatory.

"Let's just say I got my hands on her hair," Hunter said, her look absolutely wicked.

"Wow…" Kori said laughing. "And?" She couldn't stop herself from asking.

"And…it was worth the wait," Hunter said, licking her lips salaciously.

"Do you still see her?"

Hunter nodded. "Oh yeah, whenever she gets tired of her man of the week."

"So she's not gay?" Kori asked.

"Nope," Hunter said, "she says she's bisexual. She likes both."

"So you sleep with bisexual women?" Kori asked.

"I sleep with whoever grabs my interest," Hunter said, "obviously if she's interested too."

"And are a lot of women interested?" Kori asked.

Hunter grinned, her silver eyes sparkling. "Enough," she said, nodding. "A lot of times it's just an adventure for some women."

"An adventure?" Kori asked, shocked. "And that's okay with you?"

19

Hunter grinned again, shrugging. "Doesn't matter to me why a woman wants me, as long as she does, we're good to go."

"That casually?" Kori asked then.

"I told you that I'm a whore," Hunter said, her look pointed. "Did you really convince yourself that I was kidding?"

"I guess…" Kori said. "Don't you want something more serious?"

Hunter made a disgusted noise in the back of her throat. "Why?"

"Well, don't you want love?" Kori asked.

"I get what I need," Hunter said, her look serious. "Why would I want to muck that up with love?"

"Isn't love the whole point of existence?" Kori asked, sounding very philosophical.

"Not to everyone, honey," Hunter said, shaking her head. "Live fast, die young, that's my motto."

"That's really cynical, you know?" Kori said.

"I consider it realistic."

"Realistic?" Kori repeated.

Hunter looked over at Kori, canting her head. "You're married, right?"

"Yes," Kori said, nodding.

"Is it love?" Hunter asked.

"Of course," Kori said, but there was a trace of something else.

Hunter heard it and narrowed her eyes slightly. "How long have you been married?"

"Two years," Kori said.

"And you're what? Twenty? Twenty-one?" Hunter asked.

"I just turned twenty-one," Kori said.

Hunter nodded. "High school sweethearts?" she asked with a glint in her eyes.

Kori hesitated, but then nodded.

"Uh-huh," Hunter murmured, nodding. "Bet it seemed like a good idea at the time..." She quirked her lips in a sardonic grin.

"What's that supposed to mean?" Kori asked, her tone sharp.

"Steady little sister..." Hunter said, grinning, knowing she'd hit way too close to home on that one. "I just mean that people tend to get swept up in this perfect little picture. You know—married, two point five kids, a dog, a house, a white picket fence. It's bullshit. People should do what makes them happy, not what society tells them should make them happy."

"And you think that's what I did?" Kori asked.

"I have no idea," Hunter said, "but you haven't said word one about hubby since you got here. I'm betting that was him on the phone earlier, and you didn't come back all happy and with stars in your eyes. Thinkin' the bloom is off that rose and now reality is setting in."

Kori looked over at Hunter and wondered how the hell the woman saw all of that. Yes, she and Tom were having problems. Marriage wasn't what she'd always thought it would be, and it just seemed like once the excitement of the wedding and moving into their own apartment had died down, they'd become bored with each other. Everything Hunter was saying was true, and it bugged her no end.

"So you're not interested in getting married and having kids?" Kori asked.

"Well, since gays can't get married at this point...No," Hunter said, smiling smugly.

"Okay, but you can commit to someone, can't you?" Kori asked.

"But why would I want to do that?" Hunter said. "I'm having a good time, living my life and doing my own thing. Why tie myself to one person?"

"Because that's what adults do, Hunter," Kori said.

Hunter gave a short laugh, shaking her head. "No, it's what uptight, middle-class people do, babe, and it's not my thing. Thanks."

"You're saying I'm uptight?" Kori asked.

"I'm seeing a lot of tension around your mouth, and I'm also sensing a very definite brainwash in the love and marriage department," Hunter said.

"I'm not brainwashed!" Kori snapped. "I just think that people need to commit to things and other people."

Hunter chuckled. "Well, I'd rather avoid being committed to that particular institution."

"Impossible!" Kori said, throwing up her hands.

"Nah, just not willing to convert," Hunter said, her smile telling Kori that she wasn't in the least bit offended by the direction of the conversation.

In truth, Kori knew that she was very much into commitment because her parents had been together forever and seemed so happy. Her mother had told her over and over again that love wasn't instant, it was something that grew over time. So she knew if she hung in there with Tom she would eventually feel the love her parents felt for each other. It was what she'd always wanted.

When they reached the bar, Hunter got out and walked around to open Kori's door for her. Kori looked up in surprise.

22

"What?" Hunter asked.

"I just…" Kori began, then shook her head. "Nothing." She didn't want to sound even more stupid when she told Hunter that Tom had never opened a door for her, so she kept her mouth shut.

She got out of the car and followed Hunter into the bar. Hunter was greeted by a number of people and she introduced Kori to many of the patrons. They grabbed a seat near the door. The bar itself was located inside an old Victorian-style house with wood floors and all sorts of car paraphernalia on the walls. It was a nice night, so the windows were open.

The waitress walked up to their table, handing Hunter a bottle of beer and looking at Kori.

"What did you want to order, hon?" she asked, snapping her gum as she waited for Kori's answer.

"Um, just water for now," Kori said.

"Okay," the waitress answered and sauntered away.

Kori glanced over at Hunter and saw that she was canting her head to watch the waitress's behind. Hunter turned to Kori and saw the look she was getting. She grinned unrepentantly.

"I warned you…" Hunter told her.

"I know, I know," Kori said, holding up her hand in surrender.

They chatted about random topics, and Hunter eventually got her to order an actual drink.

"It's called a what?" Kori asked, aghast.

"A slippery nipple," Hunter said, grinning widely. "It's good, just try it!"

Kori shook her head, looking at the creamy liquid in the large shot glass. Putting it to her lips she tasted it. Her eyes widened.

"Oh my God, it's so good!" she exclaimed.

"Told you!" Hunter said, winking at the waitress as she dropped a twenty on her tray. "Thanks babe, keep 'em coming and put them on my tab."

"You got it, Hunter," the waitress said, smiling brightly at the tip.

"Now there is alcohol in there," Hunter cautioned Kori, "so go a little bit easy, okay?"

"Okay," Kori said nodding, even as she sipped at the drink again.

Hunter looked at the girl for a long moment, then shook her head slowly. Somehow she knew she was going to be seeing the drunk side of Kori that night. She realized she was interested in seeing exactly what that looked like.

"Okay, I'm going to go out and smoke for a minute, are you okay?" Hunter asked.

"You smoke?" Kori asked, surprised.

"Socially," Hunter said, grinning.

"I see," Kori said, nodding as she finished her first drink. She looked toward the waitress who was already bringing the next. "I'll be right here."

"And drunk as a skunk inside an hour…" Hunter muttered under her breath as she grinned.

Outside, Hunter leaned against a post on the front porch of the house; lighting a cigarette, she took a deep drag and exhaled slowly. As she smoked, two women walked up to the outside of the bar.

"What's it like in there?" one of the women, a petite blonde, asked.

"Like a bar," Hunter said, grinning indolently.

The woman who'd asked the question laughed softly. "Are you from here?" she asked, her look direct.

"I am," Hunter said, nodding, her silver eyes sparkling with interest.

"What's good around here?" the woman asked, her look changing slightly.

The slow, seductive smile that spread over Hunter's lips was unmistakable. The blonde licked her lips and sauntered up the stairs to the porch. Hunter moved to open the door for her and her friend, her cigarette clenched between her teeth.

"Thank you," the blonde said, reaching up to run a red fingernail over Hunter's jawline seductively.

"Any time," Hunter replied, her eyes sparkling again.

When Hunter rejoined Kori, she noted the two women, the blonde and her redheaded friend, were sitting at the bar. No sooner had Hunter seated herself when the waitress arrived with a beer and a note on a napkin. Hunter read the note and grinned, stuffing it into her shirt pocket as she lifted the bottle of beer, and inclined her head to the blonde who was watching her.

"What was that all about?" Kori asked, sounding a bit drunk. Hunter noted that she had three shot glasses in front of her.

"Didn't I tell you to take it easy?" Hunter asked, grinning.

"Don't avoid the question," Kori said, her green eyes somewhat glassy.

"It's just her name, the name of her hotel, and room number," Hunter said, smirking.

"That fast?" Kori asked looking over at the blonde who'd walked in while Hunter had been outside.

"So that's your type?" Kori asked.

Hunter grinned at the slight slur in Kori's words. "How drunk are you?"

"I'm buzzing pretty good," Kori said, smiling as she nodded.

"Uh-huh," Hunter said, her look open.

"So?"

"She's my type, yeah…" Hunter said, nodding.

"So you like 'em all girlie and stuff?" Kori asked.

Hunter chuckled. "I prefer femmes, yes."

"Femmes?" Kori asked, her look wavering slightly.

"Yes, the ones that are all *girlie and stuff*," Hunter said with a grin.

"Oh, so like me?" Kori said, putting her hand on her chest.

Hunter looked back at her for a long moment, then nodded slowly. "Like you, yes."

"So you really do think I'm hot?" Kori asked, her voice holding a note of wonder to it.

Hunter laughed out loud at that one, nodding as she lifted the beer to her lips again and taking a long drink. "Yeah, I think you're pretty hot."

"Ha!" Kori exclaimed, like she'd just solved some great mystery.

Another hour and two more shots for Kori later, the blonde and her friend were headed for the door. The blonde looked over at Hunter.

"Am I going to see you later?" she asked.

Hunter's lips tugged in a grin. "I gotta get her back to our base camp…" she said regretfully.

"I'm here all week," the woman said, her eyes screaming a come-on that couldn't be missed.

"Then maybe I'll see you tomorrow," Hunter said, smiling.

"Great!" the woman said, winking at Hunter, then she and her friend left.

One of the older men in the bar gave a sharp whistle. "Score another one for the Briggs family charm!" he exclaimed as a round of applause started for Hunter.

Hunter laughed, shaking her head.

"What did he mean by that?" Kori asked Hunter on the drive back to the camp an hour later. "The Briggs family charm?"

Hunter glanced over at Kori, seeing that she was still very drunk. She shrugged.

"My family has lived in this area for generations. Some of us have been rather proliferate and known to be Casanovas," she explained.

"Ah-ha!" Kori exclaimed. "So that's what you are? A Casanova?"

"I guess to some people, yeah," Hunter said, looking amused.

"You don't think you are though?" Kori asked. "I mean, sheesh, that woman didn't even know your name and she wants you to come to her hotel?"

"Some women just want hot sex, Kor. I know it doesn't jibe with your commitment scenario, but it's a fact."

"And is that what you give them?" Kori asked, her words slightly slurred.

"I don't hear too many complaints," Hunter said evenly.

"Hmmm..." Kori murmured, her look speculative.

"What?" Hunter asked, glancing over at her.

"I just don't know what that would be like," Kori answered, her look confused suddenly.

"What what would be like?" Hunter asked, trying to follow Kori's erratic thought processes.

"Hot sex with a woman," Kori said, her tone indicating her confusion.

"Well, if you've never had sex with a woman, it's understandable that you wouldn't know what it would be like," Hunter said reasonably.

"But I'm wondering if I should find out," Kori said, a grin spreading over her lips. "And I would bet you're a damned good kisser..."

"Oh ho..." Hunter said her tone indicating her shock and amusement. "I think someone's had way too much to drink and needs to sleep it off."

"You think it's the alcohol?" Kori asked.

"I know it's the alcohol, honey."

"I thought you were really hot that first day I met you," Kori said, proud of herself for admitting that.

Hunter was highly amused and she licked her lips. "Okay..." she said, nodding indulgently. "And that made the grand leap to wanting to fuck me tonight without alcohol in play?" she asked, her tone highly cynical.

Kori's eyes widened at the word 'fuck' being used to blatantly, however she felt a thrill go through her as she thought about what Hunter had just said.

"Maybe," Kori said, her tone far from sure.

"Uh-huh, okay," Hunter murmured, a sardonic grin on her lips.

She expected Kori to pass out any minute now. She was wondering exactly how much the girl weighed and if she was going to be able to carry her into the bunk house. That was right about the time Kori decided to shift forward and slide her hand over Hunter's thigh, which had Hunter swerving the car as she jumped in response.

"Holy fuck!" Hunter exclaimed. "Are you trying to get us both killed?"

Kori had practically jumped back into the passenger seat, looking terrified.

"I'm sorry," Kori said miserably, her face contrite.

Hunter had to wait until she could get her heart out of her throat, then she reached over and smoothed her thumb over Kori's cheek.

"You surprised me," she said. "I'm sorry I yelled."

"I'm sorry I surprised you," Kori said, looking embarrassed now. And then a different look took over, one which Hunter recognized.

Once again, she swerved the car to the nearest clearing, this time on purpose. She leaped out of the car and ran around to open the door for Kori, helping her to the edge of the clearing furthest from the road so she could throw up. Hunter held her hair back and rubbed her back while she retched repeatedly. When Kori finally finished losing everything in her stomach, Hunter sat on the ground, holding Kori. Kori leaned her head back against Hunter's shoulder, feeling weak.

"You okay?" Hunter asked gently.

Kori nodded slowly, still feeling as though the world spinning.

"I'm sorry…" she said softly, starting to get teary-eyed.

"You're okay," Hunter said, putting her cheek against Kori's temple. "As long as you didn't ralph in my car…" she added with a grin.

Kori laughed softly. "That's what really matters, right?"

"Right."

The next morning, Kori woke with the worst hangover of her life. It was 11 a.m. when a splitting headache pulled her out of her dreams. She turned over to see a glass of water, two aspirins, and a note from Hunter.

Take these and sleep for another two hours, you'll feel better. Be back later. ~H~

Kori read the note, grinned, and did as the note said. She woke later that afternoon feeling much better.

Hunter reappeared in camp later that evening, walking into the bunk house just as Kori emerged from the shower with a towel wrapped around her.

"Oops!" Kori said, grimacing. "I didn't know when you'd be back…" She grabbed her bathrobe and slid it on.

Hunter chuckled. "Well, I'm back," she said, moving to get her stuff together for a shower.

"Did you go back over to Mendo?" Kori asked, her look pointed.

Hunter grinned, nodding.

"Uh-huh…" Kori murmured. "Did you have a good time?"

"Oh yeah…" Hunter said, her grin widening.

"The blonde right?" Kori asked, testing her memory of the night before.

Hunter nodded, her silver eyes sparkling.

"Or was it the redhead?" Kori asked then.

Hunter simply picked up her bathroom bag and walked by Kori, leaning in as she whispered, "Both," and continued into the bathroom.

"What!" Kori exclaimed, and heard Hunter laughing behind the door. "Jesus, you really are a whore, aren't you?"

"I believe I told you that," Hunter called through as the shower turned on. "So you look like you feel good, not too hungover?" She stepped into the shower.

"Oh yeah," Kori said, walking into the bathroom to take the second towel out of her hair, making a start on picking out her long, wavy tresses. "That aspirin thing worked like a charm. Thanks for that."

"I've been there enough times to know what works," Hunter said from the shower.

"I even felt good enough to go for a nice long hike, it was great."

"Uh... Kor?" Hunter said, her tone cautionary.

"What?"

"You have read the reports about a few male black bears getting a bit aggressive out in the demo forest, right?"

"Uh..." Kori stammered, grimacing at her reflection, even as Hunter's head poked around the curtain.

"Kor?" she queried, seeing Kori's grimace. "Jesus! Don't do that again without me, okay?"

Kori squeezed her eyes shut. "Sorry!"

31

"You will be sorry if you run into one of those black bears!" Hunter said. "I mean they're not grizzlies by any means, but they can still be over two hundred pounds of mad if you run into the wrong one. And we've had a few close calls in the last few months. You gotta pay attention to the bulletins, okay?"

"Okay," Kori said, knowing that Hunter was just looking out for her, but still feeling stupid.

Winter set in to Mendocino early that year, lashing the coast with storm after storm. Cal Fire spent a lot of time rescuing people from rising water and mudslides. Kori and Hunter fell into their bunks on numerous occasions too exhausted to even talk. When they did have coinciding time off, they hung out and talked about anything and everything.

One day in December when the squad boss was on vacation and Hodge was in charge, Hunter had the day off when Kori didn't. Kori got stuck on a training exercise with Hodge and a number of the other guys. A big storm was headed in and the crew was practicing search and rescues. They'd been having problems with the radios all day and there seemed to be an issue with the transmitter at base camp. Finally, the radios were abandoned and they transitioned to yelling to each other as they moved through the forest.

As it could on the coast, the weather moved in quick—suddenly trees were swaying mightily, the wind whipping at them. Rain began pouring down and Hodge called the exercise to an end, telling everyone to head back to the trucks parked at the edge of the forest. As everyone piled into the motors, no one noticed that Kori wasn't among them, assuming in the confusion that she was in another vehicle.

Hunter got back to camp an hour after they did, hearing about how fast the weather had come up when she checked in at the office. When she got to their bunk house she was surprised not to find Kori there. She went to the chow hall and checked other areas of the camp, finally going to see Hodge.

"Where's Stanton?" Hunter asked Hodge.

"What am I? Her babysitter?" Hodge snapped, still very adversarial when it came to the 'girls' in the group.

Hunter looked back at him in disgust. "No, you're her fucking acting squad boss, moron! Where is she?"

Hodge looked wholly unconcerned as he shrugged.

"Fucking piece of shit…" Hunter muttered as she stormed out of his office.

After a number of conversations Hunter determined that they'd actually left Kori out in the test forest. Hunter was spitting mad and ready to kill Hodge. She ran back to the bunk house and quickly changed out of her dress boots into her combat boots, remaining in the slacks and long-sleeved shirt she'd been wearing earlier. Pulling off her leather jacket, she tossed it aside and pulled on her rain slicker. She grabbed her hunting knife and strapped it on, then grabbed her gear bag.

Outside she stormed to one of the trucks in the yard, throwing her gear bag into it as she got in. Hodge made the mistake of trying to stop her.

"Where do you fucking think you're going, Briggs!" he yelled over the sound of the wind.

"I'm going after her, you chicken shit!" Hunter yelled back.

"Stand down! That's an order, Briggs!" Hodge yelled.

"Fuckin' fire me!" Hunter yelled back, climbing the truck and slamming the door.

Hodge had to jump out of the way as she started the engine with a roar and accelerated out of the yard, spraying Hodge with mud as she did.

At the edge of the forest she parked and climbed out of the truck, pulling her gear bag around her shoulders. The rain was coming down in sheets and the wind was whipping it into her face. Even so, she started yelling for Kori at the top of her lungs. She walked in the direction she'd been told Kori had been headed in, cursing Hodge for his ineptitude. It was predicted to get down to freezing that night, and the icy rain would turn to snow before long. If Kori stayed out in the storm overnight she'd be in serious trouble—she could freeze to death, and Hunter wasn't going to let that happen.

It took another full hour before she started seeing the grooves on the trees. Kori had apparently learned something from her: she'd learned to mark her path so she knew where she'd been.

"Good girl, Kori!" Hunter exclaimed feeling elated suddenly—she'd started to lose hope until that moment.

She followed the markings for another punishing hour, and finally found Kori huddled under a tree, shivering violently. Running to her, Hunter grabbed her up in her arms and held onto her tightly.

"Hunter?" Kori queried wondrously.

"Fancy meeting you here," Hunter said, grinning down at her. "Let's get back to the truck, okay?"

"I hurt my ankle…" Kori said, her voice tremulous.

"Okay, well, we can handle that," Hunter said, setting her gear bag down and pulling out an Ace bandage. She quickly wrapped Kori's ankle and pulled her boot back on, lacing it loosely. "Okay, let's get you up," she said after pulling on her gear bag again.

Hunter helped Kori to her feet. "Can you put weight on it?"

Kori put her foot down and leaned on it, pulling it back up quickly. "It hurts, but I can put some on it."

"Okay, well, put your arm around my shoulders," Hunter said, bending to let Kori do that.

"So damned tall…" Kori muttered with a grimace.

"Sorry," Hunter said as they started to walk back the way Hunter had come. "They grow us redwoods tall this side of the forest," she said with a grin.

They were halfway to the truck when Hunter noticed the black bear blocking their path.

"Son of a…" Hunter muttered as she backed up, moving toward a tree. Her eyes were fixed on the bear who was regarding them tensely. "Easy big guy…" she said, guessing that it was indeed a male due to its size and wider head.

"Oh my God…" Kori breathed.

Hunter continued to back up slowly and the bear moved forward, swatting the ground with his front paws and snorting.

"Easy…" Hunter said calmly, as she started to ease Kori to the ground slowly.

"What are you doing?" Kori whispered, sounding as terrified as she felt.

"Kor, I need to challenge him to scare him off, but I need both of my arms to do that…" Hunter explained carefully as the bear edged closer.

35

With Kori on the ground near a tree, Hunter, still crouched, pulled her knife out of its sheath. Turning just in time, she noticed the bear move to his haunches, barely a foot from her. She had the forethought to put her left arm up above her head, blocking the first swipe, and felt the burning pain of one of his claws rip through her slicker and shirt sleeve. She stood up straight, lashing out with the knife in her right hand catching the bear's paw. Giving a loud yell as she did, she raised her arms above her head.

The bear jumped back, surprised by her sudden aggressiveness. Hunter knew enough about black bears to know that they weren't usually hostile and were easily scared by humans. She'd known to back out of his path and make sure he had a clear escape route. She knew to make herself appear larger and to scare the bear. Predictably, the bear turned and ran from the confrontation.

Hunter blew her breath out, re-sheathing her knife as she turned back to Kori.

"Hunter! Are you okay?" Kori asked, grabbing at her as she kneeled next to her.

"I'm fine, he just scratched me," she told Kori, then moved to help her up again. "Let's get back to the truck, before he comes back with friends, okay?" she said with a grin, knowing it wasn't likely, but wanting to calm Kori with the joke.

"Oh my God, could he?" Kori asked, panicked.

"No, babe, I was just kidding. He's gone, but we need to get out of this cold. So come on."

They made their way back to the truck as the rain began dumping in earnest, the wind growing stronger. In the truck, Hunter started the vehicle, turning the heater up full blast. She reached behind the seat and grabbed her leather jacket, putting it around Kori's shoulders. She then pulled off her slicker and took of the blue shirt she wore off, ripping off a sleeve and wrapping it around the arm that was still dripping blood, tying it off with her teeth.

"Is your arm okay?" Kori asked, looking worried.

"It's fine," Hunter said, nodding.

Hunter drove out of the clearing and got onto Highway 20 that would take them back to camp. Rain lashed the windshield and the windows were fogging up faster than the heater could clear them. Fortunately, Hunter saw the downed tree blocking the highway in time to slam on the brakes. The truck skidded to a stop.

"Fuck!" Hunter yelled. "One of those fucking days, all day long..." she muttered as she turned the truck around glancing over at Kori. "You okay over there?" she asked, seeing how violently Kori was shivering.

Kori nodded.

"We'll just go down to Fort Bragg to my mom's inn, okay?" Hunter said as she drove.

Kori nodded again.

It was another twenty minutes before Hunter's day just got worse. A rockslide had blocked the highway to the west, too.

"We're like rats in a trap..." Hunter muttered. She looked over at Kori. "Looks like we're camping tonight."

Hunter found a clearing, judging it somewhere they'd be less likely to be hit by a falling tree or a mudslide. She left the truck running, and turned the heater to blow in the cab.

"Okay, I'm not going to be able to leave this on all night, it's only got a quarter tank of gas," she said. "I guess next time I decide to conduct a rescue I should grab a truck with a full tank, huh?"

Kori laughed softly, nodding.

Hunter rummaged in her gear bag. She pulled out a pair of sweats and a T-shirt and a towel.

"We both need to get out of these wet clothes," Hunter said, her tone all business. "Put these on." She handed the T-shirt and sweats to Kori.

"What are you going to do?" Kori asked, her voice gravelly. "You need something dry too. Take the sweats at least and your jacket," she said as she started to take it off.

"You keep the jacket and the shirt, I'll take the sweats," Hunter said. "Either way we're gonna have to combine body heat… so it's about to get real sexy in here," she said with a joking wink.

Kori laughed, knowing that Hunter was trying to help her cope and appreciating it.

"I knew I'd get you naked eventually!" Kori exclaimed, laughing as she took off Hunter's jacket and pulled off her wet clothes. Leaving on her underwear, she shrugged into Hunter's T-shirt.

Hunter did the same, pulling the sweatpants on, leaving her sports bra on.

"Here, use this to try and dry your hair some," Hunter said, handing Kori the towel after she'd rubbed her barely shoulder-length hair with it.

Kori did her best to dry her hair as much as possible, putting one of the vents on it and rubbing at it with the towel.

They ended up lying facing each other on the bench seat of the truck, with Hunter's jacket and their slickers over them. Hunter had her injured arm over Kori's waist, her other arm under Kori's head, her own head on the balled-up damp towel.

"So…" Hunter said, her tone suave. "You come here often?"

Kori chuckled. "Well, I try not to get lost in the forest too much…" she said, her voice trailing off as she grimaced. "I'm sorry," she said then, "I don't know how I got so turned around and then everyone was gone…"

"I know, Hodge—that asshole—didn't even know you weren't at camp."

Kori pressed her lips together. "I'm sorry you had to risk your life to come out here to find me." Then she added, "My own personal bear hunter…"

Hunter chuckled at that title. "Bear hunter, huh? I'm not sure a game of tag really qualifies me as a 'hunter' you know."

"It does in my book," Kori said. "Seriously, though, thank you."

"Can't lose the only other girl in camp," Hunter said, winking at her. "Besides, you're kinda cute."

Kori smiled sadly. "You used to think I was hot,.

"I still think you're hot, you just look like a drowned rat right now," Hunter said, grin in place.

"Oh, I see," Kori said, "I'm only hot when I'm all made up, huh?"

Hunter smiled widely. "Now did I say that?"

"Uh-huh," Kori muttered, "And this was your day off…did you score? You looked nice enough when you left."

"I wasn't looking to score today," Hunter told her. "I had to help my mom host some people at the inn."

"You still need to take me there," Kori told Hunter.

"Yeah, yeah," Hunter said, grinning, "we've been a bit busy lately."

"I know, but still," Kori said.

Kori had been telling Hunter that she wanted to meet her family, having heard a lot about them in the last few months.

"Okay, gonna turn this off now," Hunter said, reaching out to turn the key to shut the truck off. "I want to save what gas we have left for later tonight when it gets colder."

"Okay," Kori said, nodding. Snuggling closer to Hunter, she rested her head against Hunter's chest. "How it is possible that you still smell good?"

Hunter chuckled. "Don't be making a pass at me, missy."

"Oh, that's not a pass," Kori said, her green eyes looking up at Hunter, "this is a pass."

With that, she leaned up to kiss Hunter's lips. There was a moment frozen in time, where their lips met and nothing else mattered, but then realization hit. Hunter was stunned by the desire that slammed into her instantly. It had her gripping at Kori's waist, pulling her closer as she deepened the kiss. She felt Kori shudder against her and pulled back to look at her. Kori's hand at the back of her head pulled her in as their lips met again. Things got heated quickly, but then Hunter pulled back.

"Kor, wait, wait…" Hunter breathed, her voice laced heavily with desire.

"What? Why?" Kori asked, sounding befuddled.

Hunter looked down into her eyes. "If we're gonna do this, it's not going to be here in this truck in the middle of a storm while we try not to die from exposure," she said, her look direct, "I want this to be more of a controlled burn."

"Controlled burn, huh?" Kori asked, smiling.

"Oh yeah, a nice slow one," Hunter said, grinning, her silver eyes widening slightly.

"I was right about one thing, though," Kori said as she settled her head back against Hunter's chest.

"What's that?" Hunter asked.

"You are a damned good kisser," Kori said, grinning.

"Oh honey, I'm good at everything…" Hunter said, making Kori shudder again.

Chapter 2

Kori stood looking around her office, unable to believe she was really there. Director? Holy crap! Midnight Chevalier had personally appointed her. She'd been with Cal Fire, formerly CDF, for over twenty years now and had worked her way up through the ranks. From probationary firefighter through to Region Chief for the Southern Region—which she'd been for four years now. She'd been surprised to be offered the Director's job; she knew someone else was more qualified and she was inclined to think that that someone had been offered the job first. Regardless, Kori was the director now and she needed to start looking around herself to see what she needed to do first.

***

It had been a month since she'd seen the butterfly in their bedroom. Hunter had hoped to see it again, but that hadn't happened. However, Heather had made her presence known more than once since then in small ways. The most recent hint Heather had dropped, quite literally, on Hunter's head.

Hunter had been rummaging in the hall closet for one of her jackets and something had fluttered down from the top of the

42

closet. It was a leaflet from a local realtor. Hunter had crumbled it up and thrown it in the trash. Later that week when she'd taken out the trash the balled-up leaflet fell out of the bag. Hunter had leaned down to pick it up and stuffed it back into the bag. At the outside fire pile for trash, the leaflet had fallen out again. Hunter had narrowed her eyes at the leaflet, putting it back onto the pile. The following weekend when she'd burned the trash, once again the balled-up leaflet had found its way out of the pile.

"Okay, babe, I hear you…" Hunter had finally said, rolling her eyes.

While she'd been sick, Heather had insisted that Hunter sell the house while it was a seller's market.

"You could make a million easy on this house, Hunter…" Heather had told her.

"And go where, babe?" Hunter had asked, her stomach churning at the thought of selling the house they'd bought together. "This is our home."

Heather's lips had trembled, and Hunter knew that it was because she'd thought about what they'd face in months to come. Heather had terminal cancer, and everyone knew her days were numbered. It was still hard for the family to accept.

"I mean when I'm gone, Hunter…" Heather had said, tears in her eyes.

Hunter had shaken her head vehemently, tears gathering in hers as she'd swallowed convulsively. "No, don't say that," she'd said, still wanting to deny the diagnosis and second opinion—it couldn't be real.

43

It took another couple of weeks for the idea to take hold, and Hunter had finally contacted a realtor, the one on the leaflet. She still wasn't sure it was what she wanted to do, but she wanted to at least check into it, since Heather seemed rather insistent.

"Hope you're happy now…" Hunter said, laying on their bed, staring up at the ceiling.

"What?" Samantha said as she stood in the doorway.

"I was talking to your mother," Hunter said.

"You're doing that a lot these days…" Samantha said as she walked in and sat down on the bed, looking up at her mom.

"Well, she seemed pretty damned insistent on my listing the house, so I was simply making sure she was happy that I'm talking to a realtor." Hunter rubbed her face. "I don't need a brick from the fireplace to fall on my head next," she muttered.

Samantha laughed. They'd both come to accept that Heather was still with them in one way or another, and it leant them both a great deal of comfort.

"So are you still headed down to Sacramento tomorrow morning?" Samantha asked.

"Yeah…why?"

"I was hoping I might be able to go down with you," Samantha said.

"For?"

"I want to check out some colleges there and in San Francisco," Samantha said.

Hunter drew in her breath, then nodded. "Yeah, you can come with me, is that going to be okay with school, though? I'm gone for like three or four days and I'm driving not flying."

44

"Why aren't you flying?" Samantha asked, surprised by this information.

Hunter almost always used her helicopter whenever she had to go too far south.

"There's a nasty series of storms headed in either Tuesday or Wednesday, and I don't want to get caught in them in the 'copter."

"Oh, okay," Samantha said, nodding. "Are you taking the El Camino?" she asked hesitantly.

Hunter chuckled. "No, babe, I'm taking the Lexus. Why? 'Cause you don't like the El Camino?"

"I love the El Camino, Mom, I just…Well, it doesn't have an iPod jack or anything and you know radio reception sucks between here and Sacramento."

"I know, I know," Hunter said, laughing, knowing it was her fault that Samantha was so addicted to music—she'd gotten it from Hunter early on in her life.

"Cool, so can I go?" Samantha asked.

"Sure, babe, if you're okay with staying in a hotel room with your mother."

"Mom was the one that snored, you're okay," Samantha said, chuckling.

Hunter laughed. "Careful, she'll make ya drop something if you piss her off."

Hunter had already found that out one morning when she'd been really letting her anger run over the death of her wife. She'd been cussing at fate and just about any other deity that came to mind. Her Cal Fire mug that she'd been holding had suddenly slipped from her grasp and hit the floor, splashing coffee all over her uniform. It had been a mess. That morning, Hunter had realized that her wife, dead or not, still didn't like her cussing.

The next morning at 4 a.m., Hunter woke up and got dressed. Her mind ran through all possible scenarios of running into Kori at the Fiscal System training she was headed to. It was a new system all state agencies were going to and attendance at their model office workshop was mandatory for all Cal Fire managers and above.

She knew without a doubt that she was going to run into Kori there. She was unaccountably nervous about the meeting. As the Northern Region Chief, Hunter had seen Kori over the years, but they'd never spoken to each other and had managed to stay on opposite sides of whichever room they were in. Hunter wasn't sure if that practice would continue or not. As the director, Kori would need to communicate with the Chiefs under her direction, and Hunter was one of them.

It irritated Hunter when she realized she was dressing with more care than she normally would for training. She'd put on black slacks and a dress shirt, but looking in the mirror at herself she made a disgusted noise in the back of her throat.

"Who are you trying to kid?" she said to her own reflection.

She'd promptly changed into jeans and a Cal Fire Mendocino hooded sweatshirt, adding her usual combat boots, thick black banded watch, as well as a black leather band on her left wrist. She still wore on her left ring finger the platinum band Heather had placed there almost seventeen years ago. Alongside that, Hunter added a platinum ring with a rainbow of channel set gemstones in it that Heather had gotten her their last anniversary. The final piece she put on was a silver ring with a Fleur-de-lys—a nod to Hunter's French heritage.

"Now that's more like it…" Hunter said to herself, checking her hair in the mirror.

She noted that it was growing back nicely, but she was keeping it short now, just letting the top grow out by a couple of inches so she could mess with it a bit. She'd shaved her head when Heather had started losing hers due to the intense chemotherapy she was undergoing. Heather had been mad at her for a couple of days but had finally admitted that she loved Hunter more for the support she was showing.

Regardless of the change of clothes, Hunter still felt her nerves jumping constantly. Her hands were shaking as she heated up her coffee. It was the first thing Samantha noticed too.

"You seem jumpy this morning…" Samantha observed.

Hunter's lips twitched as she did her best to pour her coffee into the mug without spilling it everywhere.

"You're gonna burn yourself!" Samantha said, moving to take the mug and glass pitcher out of her mother's hands.

"You sound exactly like your mother right now, you know that right?" Hunter said, leaning against the counter, regarding her daughter with her arms folded in front of her chest.

She saw Samantha smile fondly. "I like that."

Hunter smiled too. She loved that Samantha was a lot like Heather, but it hurt sometimes too: it was a reminder of what she'd lost. She watched as Samantha poured the coffee and twisted the top on the cup, rinsing out the pitcher and setting it in the drying rack next to the sink, exactly as Heather had so many mornings when Hunter was headed to work. Turning, Samantha handed the cup to Hunter.

"Thank you," Hunter said, smiling at her daughter.

"You're welcome, now tell me why you're so on edge."

Hunter laughed. "Just like your mother, you never let anything go…"

"Nope," Samantha said.

"It's a long story, babe." Hunter said.

"Well, we have a four-hour drive," Samantha said, smiling, "so let's go."

In the car, Hunter plugged in her phone and music filled the car. She listened to a lot of classic rock with other random songs thrown in. 'Heather' songs as she called them. They were songs that Heather either loved, or had shared with Hunter, or simply ones that reminded Hunter of Heather. One such song started shortly after they'd gotten on the road and Samantha could see tears gather in Hunter's eyes and slide down her cheeks, even though she did her best to hide them.

The song was by Sia, called 'Angel by the Wings.' The chorus was heartbreaking when applied to their loss. It talked of begging an angel for one more day and asking for the strength to stay in that life.

Samantha found that her eyes welled with tears as well. Hunter glanced over and, seeing that Samantha was crying, she reached over to take her daughter's hand and squeezed it gently. They listened to the song in silence, the cabin of the car lit by the soft blue of the dashboard lights.

When the song ended they were both quiet for a bit. Hunter picked up her coffee cup, taking a drink, doing her best to get rid of the lump in her throat.

It was a few more minutes before Samantha looked over at Hunter.

"So why are you on edge?" she asked. "Is it about this trip?"

Hunter smiled then nodded.

"What's the haps, Mom?"

Hunter chuckled. "I'm just likely to run into someone I used to know and I'm not really sure how it's going to go."

"Why?" Samantha asked. "Is this like an old adversary or something?"

Hunter's lips curled in a grin that Samantha recognized.

"Oh-ho…" Samantha exclaimed. "So not an adversary…A lover maybe?"

Hunter blew her breath out, nodding her head. She and Heather had never lied to Samantha: when she'd asked questions they were always honest with her.

"Wow!" Samantha said, smiling brightly. "Okay, so obviously before Mom…" she said, her voice trailing off as she contemplated the possibilities. "You were, what…twenty-seven when you and Mom got together, so this was before then…"

Hunter grinned at her daughter's examination of the situation. She loved that Samantha didn't think for a second that this could be someone Hunter had been with after Heather or while Heather and she had been together. It meant that Samantha knew how much she loved her mother, and that was important to Hunter.

"I was twenty-four, she was someone I worked with," Hunter said.

"Okay…" Samantha said, letting her voice trail off to encourage Hunter to say more. When Hunter didn't, she looked over at her, canting her head. "Was she cute?"

"Oh yeah, she was cute," Hunter said, nodding with a warm smile.

"Oh she was hella cute from the look of that smile!" Samantha said. "What did she look like?"

Hunter looked back over at her daughter, then shook her head, rolling her eyes. "Pull up the Cal Fire website on your phone."

"Okay…" Samantha said as she did. "What am I looking for?"

"Go to the 'About Us' tab, and look under 'Executive,'" Hunter said.

The first picture that appeared was Kori's. Hunter reached over to tap the photo. It came up larger, then she tapped it again, giving Samantha a pointed look.

"Holy crap! Her?" Samantha exclaimed, her eyes wide.

Hunter laughed out loud at that one, nodding her head.

"You dated the director?"

"Well, she wasn't the director then, but yeah," Hunter said. "She's the reason I have this," she said, touching the scar on her left forearm.

"You said a bear scratched you," Samantha said.

"It did, but I was out in a storm rescuing her when it happened," Hunter said.

"Whoa…" Samantha said, her eyes sparkling with interest. "So how come you didn't stick with her? You coulda been married to a director now."

"And I wouldn't be your mother," Hunter said, "or have met your mother."

"True," Samantha said, "but you wouldn't have known that then. So what happened?"

Hunter gave Samantha a measured look, then shrugged. "I wasn't really into commitment then, and…well, there were other complications."

"Like?" Samantha asked.

"Like a husband."

"Oh," Samantha said her eyes widening, "she was married? To a man?"

"Yeah," Hunter said, nodding.

"That sucks," Samantha said, then looked over at Hunter. "Is she still married to him?"

"As far as I know," Hunter said, her look complacent.

***

The morning after the storm, the crews had been able to get to them. Fortunately, by the time they got there both Kori and Hunter had been able to pull on some of their still damp clothes. Hunter's arm had been checked out by the onsite medic, who'd cleaned it and put in a couple of stitches on the deeper parts of the wound. They were both given a couple of days off to recover.

Kori had been pulled in by the squad boss who'd returned from vacation early due to the incident. She'd been questioned as to what had happened and how Hunter had located her. She'd even been asked if she wanted to file a report against Hodge for neglecting to account for her. She said she'd think about it and left it at that. On her way back to their bunk house, Kori talked to a few of the other crew members and heard some things which had her ready to question Hunter.

In their bunk house, Kori found Hunter lying on her bed on her back, her now bandaged arm up resting low across her abdomen and her other arm above her head. It was the way Kori noted Hunter slept all the time. She sat on Hunter's bunk, looking down at her. Hunter had opened her eyes the moment she'd stepped into the cabin.

"How'd that go?" Hunter asked Kori.

"Well, they said I did good with marking my path—I told them it was because you taught me that. They also want to know if I want to file a complaint about Hodge leaving me out there."

"And are you going to do that?" Hunter asked, her look intractable.

"I wanted to talk to you about it," Kori said. "What do you think I should do?"

Hunter drew in a deep breath. "I think it's up to you."

"Come on," Kori said, "you know this stuff better than me, I'm not sure if it's the smart move right now."

"Why?" Hunter asked, her look still unreadable.

"Because these guys already don't like me," Kori said, "and if I file on Hodge, they probably won't ever like me."

"Why do you care if they like you?" Hunter asked.

"Because these guys are our backup, and if they hate us they won't come for us when we need them. On top of that, I want to make CDF my career, and you never know who you're going to have to work with or for."

Hunter regarded her for a long moment, then curled her lips into a grin. "Good answer," she said, nodding.

Kori nodded too, smiling, she had thought that's what Hunter would think too. She respected Hunter's opinion, because she knew a lot more about working with and around men than Kori did.

"I heard something else..." Kori began, looking pointedly at Hunter.

"What?" Hunter asked, moving to sit up, canting her head slightly.

"That you disobeyed a direct order not to come after me," Kori said, her tone indicating how serious that could have been for Hunter.

Hunter's look barely flickered as she nodded, then she shrugged with a grin. "Yeah, but it was an order from Hodge, so that really doesn't hold much weight with me."

"It wouldn't stop them from putting you on report," Kori said.

"Don't care," Hunter said, her tone contemptuous. "I wasn't leaving you out there, Kor, it was as simple as that. And if they want to fire my ass for that, they can go right ahead."

Kori smiled warmly. "And I thanked you for that, right?"

Hunter grinned. "You did, yeah."

"Good," Kori nodded smiling.

"So, we got a couple of days on the beach..." Hunter said, reaching out to touch Kori's cheek, her silver eyes capturing Kori's gaze. "What's say we head over to Fort Bragg? You can meet my mother and we can have some"—she glanced at her watch—"dinner by the time we get there. Then we can go to my cottage."

"You have a cottage?" Kori asked, her eyes widening slightly.

"I do," Hunter said, nodding.

"That sounds great," Kori said, nodding.

An hour later they were on their way up Highway 20, winding their way through the 35 miles to Fort Bragg. The storm had blown through, downing more trees, but the road had been mercifully cleared since it was the only highway between Willits and Fort Bragg. It took them forty-five minutes the way that Hunter drove—it took other people an hour normally. Hunter had called her mother to let her know she was bringing her friend over to meet her and Maggie Briggs had happily set to cooking right away.

"I'll warn you now," Hunter said as she opened Kori's passenger-side door, "my mother cooks for an army and she will feed you. So…just get used to it."

"Got it," Kori said, grinning.

Inside the house, Maggie greeted Kori warmly. She gave Kori a tour of the inn that had been in their family for over a hundred years. Kori was in awe of its beauty and character. Hunter had walked along with them, having intimate knowledge of every room in the inn since she'd helped renovate them more than once in her lifetime.

"Hunter's so handy," Maggie said, touching her daughter on the shoulder fondly.

"I can wield a hammer with the best of them, Mom," Hunter said, grinning.

"It's more than that, Hunter Desolé Briggs, and you know it!" Maggie said.

"Desolé?" Kori queried, with a smile.

"We're French," Maggie told Kori. "Desolé was Hunter's paternal grandmother's name."

"I like it," Kori said, her smile wide, her green eyes on Hunter, who only rolled her eyes shaking her head.

Later at dinner a discussion had touched on the incident the night before, and then another had ensued over how many family members Hunter had.

"Then there's your uncle Jimmy, Hunter's dad's brother, and his three boys…and then Tommy just had twins…" Maggie was saying, tallying the numbers on her fingers. "Oh my, now I've lost count again…"

"Suffice it to say it's a damned lot," Hunter told Kori with a grin as she picked up her beer and took a drink.

"You weren't kidding about the proliferate part," Kori said, chuckling.

"No, ma'am," Hunter said. "Mom, we gotta get going." They'd already lingered an hour past dinner.

"Okay," Maggie said, "come by tomorrow, your cousins will be here."

"Which ones?" Hunter asked.

"I'm not sure I should tell you, since I see that look in your eye that says if I say the names of ones you don't like you won't come by," Maggie said, with so much sass in her tone that Hunter had to laugh.

"Right you are!" Hunter said. "As long as it's not Jillian and her brood, I'll be here."

"It's not, they're in Florida right now," Maggie said, making a face. "Whoever heard of spending Christmas in Florida?" she asked, shaking her head ruefully.

"Probably people who live in Florida, Ma," Hunter said, grinning.

"Well they don't live there!" Maggie said.

"It's a conundrum," Hunter said, smiling indulgently at her mother. Then moving to stand, she leaned over to kiss her cheek.

"Thanks for dinner, it was great as always, and now I can't eat again for a week."

"Stop that!" Maggie said. "You are far too skinny, Hunter Desolé."

"Fighting weight, Ma, fighting weight," Hunter said with a grin.

"My eye!" Maggie said, standing to hug Kori. "Glad you're both okay," she said as she kissed Kori on the cheek.

"Me too," Kori said smiling. "It was really great to meet you, Maggie."

"Call me Mom, all of Hunter's friends always do," Maggie said, "ever since she was a kid."

Kori nodded, smiling. "Okay," she said, innately pleased by the suggestion.

It was dark when Hunter drove up to the cottage. They got out of the car and Hunter walked around it, taking Kori's hand and leading her toward the house. Kori could make out very few details of the building, only noting that there were lights burning in a couple of the windows. Hunter used her keys to open the front door, then stepped inside, and turned on lights. Kori was surprised by the vaulted ceilings in the entry way, but she was quickly distracted by Hunter pulling her in close to kiss her lips.

Hunter's lips moved over hers expertly, sucking gently then pressing harder. She pulled back slightly, only to move in once more to kiss her again. Kori found herself completely undone by the kiss. Her arms wound up around Hunter's neck of their own volition, and Kori felt Hunter's hand slide around her back to pull her closer, her other hand sliding through Kori's hair almost reverently.

They stood in the entryway, kissing for what seemed like hours. Kori was beginning to understand what Hunter had meant by a controlled burn: she felt like Hunter had sparked a flame inside her and was adding fuel to it little by little. Hunter's hand made its way from Kori's hair to her jawline, her thumb stroking her cheek. Her fingers moved with feather-light touches that sent tiny waves of pleasure all through Kori's body. When Hunter's thumb brushed toward the corner of Kori's mouth, pressing Kori's lips apart as her tongue slid between them, Kori couldn't stop the moan that seemed to emanate from her core.

"Hunter please..." Kori found herself begging in a desperate whisper.

She felt Hunter grin against her lips, then she pulled back, looking down at Kori. Her eyes searched Kori's face, her look serious. Hunter nodded, as if confirming something to herself, then she dropped her hand, taking Kori's in hers again and she led her further into the house. In the master bedroom, she led Kori over to the bed and leaned in to kiss her again as she slowly took off Kori's jacket, laying it aside. One by one she unbuttoned the shirt that Kori wore, her lips leaving Kori's to trail down her neck, and then over the edges of her bra, as she exposed Kori's skin little by little.

Kori stood, breathing heavily, putting her hands into Hunter's hair and grasping at her head. She wanted to beg again but knew that it wouldn't do any good: Hunter was going at her own pace, and Kori was willing to let her do anything she wanted. Her body was so completely alive, Kori had no idea why it didn't simply fly apart from all the sensations running through it.

Hunter brushed the sides of Kori's shirt aside as she kneeled in front of Kori, her hands sliding around Kori's waist to her back, her lips on Kori's stomach. Kori could feel Hunter's thumbs brushing back and forth on her back, and then her hands moved slowly up and forward. Kori gasped out loud when she felt Hunter's thumbs brush over her nipples, hard even through the material of her bra. She felt the moist kisses Hunter was placing on her stomach, along and just above the waistline of her jeans. Kori ached to reach down and unbutton her jeans, to encourage Hunter to move lower, but she didn't dare—not wanting to interfere with Hunter's controlled burn.

Finally Hunter slid her hands down to the button on Kori's jeans, unbuttoning them and moving her lips to nuzzle just inside of the jeans. Kori's hands moved from Hunter's head, sliding down over Hunter's shoulders, her nails grazing over the material of the shirt Hunter wore. She felt Hunter shudder slightly under her hands and gasped as a tremor went through her; the simple thought that Hunter was affected by her made her ache even more. Hunter tugged on the jeans, sliding them down Kori's legs. Kori happily kicked off her tennis shoes and stepped out of the jeans, her hands still on Hunter's shoulders.

Hunter slid her hands up the back of Kori's legs, with just enough pressure to keep it from tickling, but not so much that it hurried things along. Her hands slid up the backs of Kori's thighs and sensually over her ass, her arms bent at a forty-five-degree angle, her hands against Kori's lower back, pressing Kori closer as she placed a kiss to Kori's skin just above her low bikini underwear.

"God…" Kori breathed as her body lit up anew at the sensation. Hunter's hands slid lower, touching the backs of Kori's thighs at the crease where they met her ass.

Hunter's thumbs brushed upward at the very innermost part of Kori's thighs, spreading the very sensitive skin there suggestively as her

58

lips pressed against Kori's pubic hair through her panties. Kori cried out as the orgasm ripped through her, making her shudder and quake, her hands grasping at Hunter's head and shoulders to keep from collapsing completely as wave after wave of ecstasy crashed through her. Hunter held her bucking body against her, her lips continuing to nuzzle against her core, through the panties, causing the orgasm to go on and on.

When the orgasm finally eased, Kori reached blindly behind her to touch the mattress. Hunter moved back, letting her sit down to catch her breath. When Kori opened her eyes, she saw Hunter's silver eyes staring up at her, a very satisfied smile on her lips.

"You're right, you're good at everything," Kori said breathlessly, nodding her head.

***

Hunter glanced over at Samantha as she pulled off the freeway onto an exit with a Starbucks sign proudly displayed. Samantha was asleep and had been for a while.

"Sam?" Hunter queried gently.

"Mmm?" Samantha murmured as she shifted in her seat, slowly opening her eyes and looking around. "Where are we?"

"Around Arbuckle," Hunter said.

"Jeeze, Mom! I'm sorry, I was going to be more entertaining," Samantha said.

"You snore like your mother, it *was* entertaining," Hunter said, grinning.

Samantha gave her an open-mouthed stare, then laughed. "Thanks, Mom," she said, shaking her head.

"Any time baby girl, any time," Hunter teased as she pulled into the Starbucks parking lot. "I'll make it up to you by getting you Starbucks, how's that?"

"That might work," Samantha said, smiling.

Twenty minutes later they were back in the car.

"That's why you're so skinny!" Samantha was exclaiming, complaining about how Hunter could go into a Starbucks, order a dark espresso roast coffee and put neither cream nor sugar into it and still drink it.

"Why is everyone always complaining about me being skinny?" Hunter asked.

***

The morning after their first time together, Kori woke lying next to Hunter. Hunter was lying in her usual position on her back with one arm up over her head, the other around Kori's shoulders. The sun was just barely peeking over the horizon and Kori looked around the room they were in. She saw that it was really rustic with exposed timbers on the ceiling, hardwood floors and wainscoted walls. She shifted to look around, and that's when she felt Hunter's hand tighten at her waist.

"Good morning," Hunter said, her voice gravelly from sleep.

"Good morning," Kori replied, looking up at Hunter. Then her glance moved over them both. "How is it that I'm naked and you're still wearing that?"

"Luck on my part?" Hunter queried. "If I recall correctly, you took your bra and panties off yourself."

"Okay, true," Kori said, nodding, "and all you took off was your jeans, jacket, and shoes."

60

"I was too tired to remove anything else," Hunter said.

"Mmhm..." Kori murmured, giving Hunter a narrowed look.

After her earth-shattering orgasm, Kori had sat on the bed. Hunter had gotten to her feet, removing some of her clothes and moving to lay down on the bed. She had reached up to pull Kori down with her. Kori had resisted long enough to shed her bra and panties, bending down to lie next to Hunter. They'd both fallen asleep shortly thereafter.

Kori snuggled against her, shivering as she slid her hand over Hunter's waist.

"Are you cold?" Hunter asked, looking down at her. "I can start a fire if you want..."

"Oh, that would be nice," Kori said, smiling.

Hunter climbed out of bed, and walked over to the rustic fireplace, picked up the lighter, and set it to the kindling already in place. Kori watched Hunter move, finding herself fascinated with her even more now. As Hunter turned to walk back toward the bed, she noted Kori watching her and grinned.

"What?" Hunter asked, as she sat down on the bed again.

"I think I can see why those two tourists wanted you so much..." Kori said.

"What is it you see?" Hunter asked with a curious look.

"The way you move, the way you look..." Kori said, her voice trailing off as she slid her hand up Hunter's chest, moving to lean up onto her elbows. "You have an innate confidence about you, of course I understand that now too."

Hunter chuckled. "You do, huh?"

"Oh my God, Hunter, I've never been that excited in my entire life!" Kori exclaimed. "You're an incredible lover."

"Oh honey, that wasn't even my A game," Hunter said, winking at her.

"See! That's what I'm talking about," Kori said, her green eyes gleaming like rich emeralds in the morning sunlight. "You know without a doubt what you're good at, and you exude it like a phero-mone. But it isn't just sex, it's how you teach, how you talk. Everyone knows you know what you're talking about, and they don't doubt you for a second. It's a special thing that you have, Hunter, and you have it in massive quantities."

Instead of answering what Kori had said, Hunter reached up, rubbing her thumb over the bridge of Kori's nose, and up her fore-head, her look searching.

"You are so beautiful…" she murmured, her silver eyes connecting with Kori's.

She slid her hand to the back of Kori's head, pulling her down to kiss her lips. Reaching up to bury both of her hands in Kori's hair, Hunter used her handfuls to guide her head back to her lips over and over again. Within minutes Kori was moaning softly. Hunter guided her body using her hands on Kori's hips as she pulled Kori over her, her hands caressing and smoothing over her skin. Kori writhed, feel-ing her body coiling for the inevitable orgasm—but she was surprised when Hunter shifted her weight, moving to put Kori under her body instead.

"Hunter…" Kori breathed, reaching up to grasp at Hunter's body.

Kori was actually stunned when Hunter moved her body against hers, her hips pressing against her, grinding, and exciting her further. Before long, Kori was crying out in her release, her nails biting into Hunter's waist as she grasped at the material of the other woman's tank top. Hunter shifted her weight again, moving to lay on her back, pulling Kori back over her.

Kori rested her head against Hunter's chest.

After a few minutes, she looked down at Hunter. "I'm sorry, am I squishing you?" she asked as she started to shift off of Hunter.

Hunter's hands stopped her. "No, you're not. Jeeze, what do you weigh? Like ninety pounds on a good day?"

"I weigh a hundred and one, thank you very much!" Kori said, grinning.

"Oh-ho…so fat," Hunter said, rolling her eyes.

"Hey, I'm not the one whose mother accused her of being too skinny," Kori said.

"That's 'cause my mother judges me on everyone else in my family," Hunter said, chuckling. "Most of us are fairly rounded."

"Well, what happened to you?" Kori asked, pinching Hunter's waist and finding not an ounce of fat there.

"I think I got my dad's physique," Hunter said.

Kori canted her head. "You never talk about him."

Hunter shrugged, her look distant suddenly. "He left when I was sixteen."

"Oh, that sucks," Kori said, grimacing.

"My fault really," Hunter said. "I made the mistake of coming out to him and my mom."

"I can't believe that's why he left, Hunter," Kori said, looking doubtful. "I'm sure there was more to it than that."

"Oh there was," Hunter said, with a humorless grin. "When I told them, he hit me and said that no kid of his was going to be a sick pervert. My mom told him that if that was how he really felt he needed to leave…" Her voice trailed off as she shook her head. "He left."

Kori grimaced again. "God, Hunter, I'm so sorry…that's…that's not how parents should be."

"You think your parents would be okay if you were gay?"

"Oh, I know they would be," Kori said. "My parents have always accepted me for who I am no matter what."

"That's what I thought too," Hunter said.

"Your mother adores you," Kori said, "your father was obviously stupid." She said it with so much vehemence that it made Hunter grin.

They lay silently for a few minutes. Then Kori leaned up, looking down at Hunter.

"And still you have clothes on…" she said narrowing her eyes at Hunter.

"So take them off of me," Hunter told her, silver eyes widening slightly.

Kori bit her lip but reached down to pull at the bottom of Hunter's tank top, bringing it up over Hunter's head. Hunter's body was as lean as her appearance testified to—not skinny, but all muscle.

Kori leaned down, kissing Hunter's lips, her hands reaching between them to caress Hunter's skin. Hunter moaned softly, her hands reaching up to slide through Kori's hair. When things got particularly heated again, Kori looked down at Hunter, then moved slowly down Hunter's body, grasping the boxer briefs she wore and taking them off as she did. Hunter's silver eyes watched her the entire time, a very definite fire in them, and it served to excite Kori even more.

Kori situated herself between Hunter's legs, and then slid her entire body very slowly up and through Hunter's legs, her skin making contact with a very sensitive and excited part of Hunter's body.

"Oh my God!" Hunter groaned loudly. "Kor...God..." She cried out as Kori's pelvis made contact and caused just the right friction. Hunter was coming immediately, grinding her body against Kori with such abandon that Kori came right along with her.

They both lay gasping for breath afterwards, Hunter's hands in Kori's hair, Kori's lips against Hunter's neck.

Shortly afterwards, Kori and Hunter became friends with benefits. They were friends who had sex often, although they were careful to keep it out of the camp, except for in their cabin with the door locked, as much as possible. Hunter made it abundantly clear that she wasn't interested in breaking up Kori's marriage, and Kori understood that. They spent a lot of time together, and Hunter taught Kori everything she knew. What Hunter didn't teach her, Kori went down to the academy in Ione to learn for herself.

During one such trip, six months after they'd started sleeping together, Hunter went into town and got to flirting with a girl in the bar. Kori had been gone for two weeks, and Hunter was getting edgy. She needed to blow off steam. The girl had wanted to see the camp, so Hunter had indulged her. It had resulted in some hot sex in the cabin, and they'd fallen asleep in Hunter's bed.

Hunter woke the next morning to the sound of someone clearing their throat. She opened her eyes to see Kori staring down at her, her lips pressed together in disapproval as her eyes skipped to the girl, then back to Hunter.

Hunter grinned unrepentantly, holding her hand up to Kori—who automatically leaned down to kiss Hunter's lips. The girl stirred then, opening her eyes and looking from Hunter to Kori as Kori went to put her stuff away. Hunter looked at the girl.

"Sorry, babe, you gotta get going," Hunter said, "my roommate is home…so…" She nodded her head toward the door.

The girl blinked a couple of times, catching the narrowed look Kori sent her. Finally she nodded and got up, pulling on her clothes as Hunter watched, grinning. The girl moved toward the door and Hunter canted her head to watch her walk, garnering a finger snap to the back of the head from Kori. She laughed.

"This was fun," the girl said, turning to look at her from the door.

"Definitely," Hunter agreed, smiling.

"Bye," the girl said then.

Hunter had no sooner lay back when Kori moved to lay over her, looking down at her.

"Hi…" Hunter said, smiling up at her.

"Hi," Kori said, smiling, her green eyes narrowed slightly. Even so, she leaned down to capture Hunter's lips with hers.

Before long, Hunter had removed Kori's and they were making love, forgetting their usual rule to lock the door in their heated reunion. When they lay together afterwards trying to catch their breath, Hunter glanced toward the door and saw that the girl was standing there looking fascinated.

Hunter grinned lopsidedly, and Kori turned to look in the same direction.

"I forgot my purse," the girl said, moving to pick up the bag from the dresser. "But I can stay if you want a third…" she offered hopefully.

Kori's green eyes narrowed dangerously. "I already shared her with you more than I'd like," she almost growled..

Hunter's eyes widened, her lips curling into a grin at the possessiveness in Kori's voice. The girl took the hint and left.

Hunter looked up at Kori, who gazed down at her, her expression still serious.

"No one else has you here," Kori told her in no uncertain terms. "This is the bed you share with me and me alone."

Again, Hunter's eyes widened. Instead of answering, Hunter reached up to kiss Kori again.

Chapter 3

Hunter and Samantha finally reached Sacramento and Hunter navigated her way to the training location. They got out of the car and Hunter immediately lit a cigarette.

"I thought you were quitting," Samantha said as she looked over at her mother.

"You thought wrong," Hunter told her simply.

"Mom, wanted you to quit," Samantha pointed out.

"I know," Hunter said, nodding, even as she took a long drag, "but I need this right now, okay?" Her look was so edgy that Samantha had to nod.

"I'll walk you over to the light rail," Hunter said, as she reached into the car for her coffee. Pocketing her cigarettes and lighter, she grabbed her headphones out of the center console, putting them around her neck and sliding her phone into her back pocket.

"Let's go," Hunter said, taking her daughter's hand.

"Okay, you have the train schedule, right?" Hunter asked Samantha. "And the list of the schools you're checking out?"

"Yeah, Mom," Samantha said, putting her head on Hunter's shoulder, knowing that Hunter was worried about her. "I've got it all, I'm checking out Sac State and UC Davis here, and then

I'm gonna get on the train and go out to UC Berkley and a couple of possibilities in San Francisco."

"Okay, you have your credit card, right?" Hunter asked. "I don't want you taking any public transit after this light rail, you use Uber okay?"

"Yes, Mom," Samantha said as they reached the light rail station.

Hunter stayed with her until the train arrived, smoking the entire time. After it pulled away from the station, Hunter made the one block walk back to the building. She signed into the training and went to the room she was directed to. The training introduction had already started, so Hunter took a seat at one of the computers in the back—but not before she caught sight of Kori's long wavy blonde hair at the front of the room. It was a full class.

After the introduction, the trainers wanted everyone to introduce themselves and tell everyone their classification and where they worked. Hunter rolled her eyes. She'd been hoping to be unnoticed for as long as possible.

As it was, when they got to her and Hunter said, "Hunter Briggs, Cal Fire, North Region Chief," Kori's head snapped around instantly, her green eyes finding Hunter's. Hunter looked back at Kori for a long moment, inclined her head slightly, then leaned back in her chair.

The morning session was nothing short of painful in terms of confusion and general annoyance at the system they were all being forced into using. Hunter already knew that it was going to create huge backups for everyone, and no one was happy about it.

By the time they were released for lunch, Hunter was so completely irritated that she strode out of the classroom before they were even officially released. She stuffed her headphones into her ears, hooking them up to her phone and cranking her music. Pausing outside long enough to light a cigarette, she wondered if she could get away with beer for lunch.

Before she got to her car, she caught movement in her peripheral vision. Turning her head, she saw Kori looking back at her grinning indulgently. Hunter immediately pulled one of her headphones out of her ear and grimaced.

"Sorry," she said, as she stopped walking.

"It's okay," Kori said, smiling. Her green eyes sparkled in the sunlight. "I get the need to drown out everything that we just heard in there," she said, hooking her thumb toward the building.

Hunter chuckled, lighting another cigarette.

Kori was amazed that Hunter looked almost exactly the same as she had years before, she never seemed to change much. Her hair was much shorter, but her silver eyes still shone brightly. Her face was still lean and smooth, even though there was a definite look of sadness to her now.

"Were you headed to lunch?" Kori asked

"Yeah," Hunter said, nodding.

"Would you mind some company?" Kori asked, her tone soft and her eyes somewhat pleading.

Hunter looked back at Kori, remembering the last time she'd seen that look on Kori's face.

***

Things between Kori and Hunter had gone along smoothly for a full year. There were a few times when Kori would go home to visit Los Angeles and find that Hunter was a bit distant when she got back, but all in all their relationship was great and comfortable for both of them. Kori met much more of Hunter's family and everyone loved her. They were forever telling Kori she should just grab Hunter and run away. Hunter always shook her head, telling whichever relative it was that Kori was happily married. Kori never bothered to correct Hunter—it didn't matter anyway, Hunter wasn't interested in running away with her. Hunter still spent time away from her in hotel rooms with random tourists. She knew she couldn't say anything: they were 'friends', and she was married.

Then Hunter got hurt and everything changed for Kori. Kori and Hunter were on separate teams because Hunter had wanted Kori to learn from other firefighters. Hunter had recently been promoted to a Fire Apparatus Engineer and had her sights set on Squad Boss next. Kori had been holding her own and learning fast from anyone and everyone. She'd become a very important member of her team, always keeping a level head no matter what happened. It was always Kori who came up with unique ideas or plans to handle situations that arose. She had an innate ability to adapt to anything and do so quickly.

They were working a huge fire that had started near the Mendocino Headlands Park. The fire was so big it was creating its own weather, causing wind and mini fire tornados. Hunter had been working with the newest crew members, trying to teach them as they went along. Unfortunately, it had pulled her focus just enough to miss the slight shift in the wind. Suddenly, the fire was coming back on her and the three young firefighters with her.

"Run!" Hunter yelled, pointing to the quickly closing space between fires as they started to circle back on them.

The three young people made it out but Hunter, who'd recently hurt her knee during an exercise, didn't make it in time. She had to fight her way out.

Kori heard the radio call that Briggs was trapped and she was sure she felt her heart stop. She immediately started running toward the sector Hunter's team had been working. Things were frantic. Forcing herself to stay calm, Kori looked around them.

"Where is she?" she yelled to the three young firefighters she knew had been with Hunter.

One of the girls pointed in the direction and Kori felt her heart drop, seeing the flames billowing up. But as she looked she saw movement. She searched around her again.

"The dozer!" she yelled, and she ran toward it. Jumping onto it she fired it up, even as another firefighter jumped onto it. "Call for a drop!" She motioned to the other firefighter. He lifted his radio to his lips and did what she said.

To Kori it felt like forever, but as she drove the bulldozer toward the fire, she heard the helicopter that had been rerouted starting to buzz overhead.

"Drop, drop, drop!" Kori yelled into her radio.

The water drop only partially dowsed the flames, but it was enough. Kori plowed the bulldozer through the fire, lowering the bucket to hopefully give Hunter something to jump into. The moment she broke the plane of the fire, she saw Hunter. She was doing her best to battle back the flames, but was quickly running out of defensible space.

"Hunter!" Kori shouted.

Hunter's head whipped around, and Kori could see that her face was black and red from the smoke. Hunter quickly backed toward

72

the bulldozer. As soon as Hunter climbed into the scoop, Kori threw the dozer in reverse and backed out of the fire and another half mile. She lowered the scoop and Hunter all but fell out of it. Kori jumped off screaming for a medic and rushing to Hunter's side.

"Hunter!" Kori yelled, just as Hunter collapsed to the ground, her breathing labored.

The medic hurried up and checked her pulse. "She may have scorched her lungs, we gotta get her to the hospital now."

A rescue helicopter was called in, and Kori went with them. She was flown to the Mendocino Coastal District Hospital and they took Hunter into the Emergency Room immediately.

It was two hours before Kori was able to see her.

"We're watching her for any acute edema to her lungs," the doctor told her. "She's on oxygen and we've started some steroids to help with the inflammation in her throat."

"But she's going to be okay, right?" Kori asked, her tone worried.

"We're hoping so, yes," the doctor said. "Has her family been notified?"

"Yes," Kori said, nodding. "I had her mom called, someone's gone to Fort Bragg to get her. Can I see her?" Kori asked then.

"Of course," the doctor said, nodding.

In the hospital room Kori went straight to Hunter's side, and sat in the chair next to the bed. Leaning forward and looking into Hunter's face, she ran her fingers through the hair at Hunter's forehead.

Hunter's silver eyes opened, looking at her over the top of the mask. She pulled the mask down.

"Your...turn..." Hunter said, her voice gruff and hesitant.

"My turn to what?" Kori asked.

73

"Save…me…" Hunter said.

"Yeah it was my turn to save you," Kori said, smiling, her fingers stroking Hunter's hair rhythmically.

Hunter's eyes closed slowly.

Kori reached over and put the mask back on. Hunter's eyes opened after a few moments, looking at Kori, then down at Kori's hand that now rested on the bed.

"Put…that…back," Hunter said, her words muted by the oxygen mask.

"What?" Kori asked, then saw that Hunter was looking at her hand. "Here?" she asked, putting her hand back into Hunter's hair, stroking it again.

Hunter nodded, closing her eyes again.

"Okay, babe, you got it…" Kori said, feeling her heart ache at seeing Hunter so weak and disheveled.

When Maggie got to the hospital she was shown to Hunter's room, the first thing she saw was Kori sitting next to the bed, stroking Hunter's hair and talking softly to her. Walking over, she leaned down to kiss Hunter's cheek, then leaned over to kiss Kori on the forehead.

"How're my girls?" Maggie asked.

Hunter's eyes opened. Looking up at her mother, she nodded, too tired to speak.

"She'd good, Mom," Kori said, looking up at Maggie, "they're just going to keep her for a couple of days so they can make sure there's no infection that crops up from the smoke inhalation."

"Okay, good," Maggie said, nodding.

Three days later Hunter was back in her bed at the cabin, where she'd been told to stay for the next couple of days to fully recover her strength. Kori got her settled in, making sure she had everything she needed, then left for her half shift, not wanting to leave Hunter alone too long. When she got back to the cabin, Hunter was sleeping. She laid down next to Hunter, so relieved that she was alright. No infection had occurred, and the doctor said her lungs were already healing well. They'd been extremely lucky.

Hunter slept the entire night, only waking once with a coughing fit that left her exhausted. Kori soothed her back to sleep.

The next morning Kori woke, moving to sit up carefully so she didn't disturb Hunter. She stared at her friend, thinking about what had happened. She'd been terrified that she would lose Hunter, and that thought had panicked her completely. It was at that moment that she'd realized she was in love with Hunter, and she knew she needed to tell her.

Hunter had just stirred and opened her eyes when there was a knock at their cabin door.

"Yeah?" Kori called, having locked the door.

"Stanton, you have a visitor!" one of the men yelled.

"Okay!" Kori called back. "I'll be there in a minute!"

She looked back over at Hunter. "Don't run off, I'll be right back," she told her with a wink. Hunter grinned.

Kori walked out of the cabin and was completely stunned to see Tom, her husband, standing there.

"Tom, what are you doing here?" Kori asked, even as he held out his arms to her.

She walked into his arms, her thoughts panicked suddenly.

"You said your friend was hurt, I wanted to get here to support you," Tom told her.

"Oh, she's better now," Kori said, biting her lip, feeling bad that he'd gone to the trouble he had to get there. She knew it was a long three-hour ride from San Francisco.

"Well, I'd like to meet her," Tom said, smiling. "You talk about her so much."

"She's asleep right now," Kori said quickly. "I really don't want to wake her, she needs her rest."

"No problem," he said smiling tritely. "Maybe later. I'm here for three days."

"Oh..." Kori said, grimacing. "No one can stay here at the camp. Maybe you can get a hotel room in Willits."

"Didn't you say that your friend's mom owns an inn? I'd rather give her the business," Tom said reasonably.

Kori grimaced, thinking the last thing she wanted was for Hunter's mom to meet her husband, but she couldn't think of a reasonable explanation as to why he couldn't stay there.

"Okay, well, we can drive over later and see if she has room," Kori said, thinking fast. "Let me grab my jacket, I'll show you around the camp." It was the last thing she wanted to do at that point, but couldn't get out of it.

She walked back into the cabin, looking over at Hunter.

"Guess who's here," Kori said to Hunter, her look far from happy.

"Who?" Hunter asked.

"Tom," Kori said.

"Seriously?" Hunter asked looking shocked.

"Yeah," Kori said, rolling her eyes. "I'm going to go show him the camp to keep him occupied...He wants to meet you," she added with a grimace.

"Uh..." Hunter said shaking her head. "I'm not sure that's a good idea."

Kori bit her lip, nodding, having thought that would be Hunter's reaction. "I'll figure some way out of that," she told Hunter. "I'll be back, okay? You rest."

"Okay," Hunter said, nodding.

After Kori walked out, Hunter lay staring up at the ceiling, her look serious. It was one thing to know about a husband in Los Angeles, it was a whole other thing to have to meet him face to face.

In the end, Kori took Tom to Maggie's inn, and they stayed there. She did everything she could to avoid sleeping with him, but there was no way to do that—it had been six months since she'd been home. On the last day Tom was there, before Kori took him down to San Francisco, he insisted on meeting Hunter.

"Let me go make sure she's decent," Kori told Tom.

She walked into the cabin and looked around. Hunter was sitting on her bed, her headphones in her ears. She smiled when she saw Kori, but that smile faded when she saw Kori's face. Reaching up, she pulled the headphones out of her ears.

"What?" she asked.

"Tom's here, and he's insisting on meeting you," Kori said. "Will you please just meet him real quick? We can tell him you're getting ready to go on shift, so you have to go, it'll be quick I promise..." Kori's voice trailed off, her eyes pleading with Hunter. She didn't know any way out of this.

"Fine!" Hunter exclaimed, rolling her eyes.

The meeting with Tom was extremely uncomfortable for Hunter, because he seemed to be a genuinely nice guy. He was average looking, with kind, brown eyes. Hunter felt like shit for hours after she met him. He even thanked her profusely for rescuing Kori way back in the beginning. It looked like he sincerely loved Kori and it only made Hunter feel worse.

***

"Am I allowed to say no to the director?" Hunter asked, grinning at Kori.

"I'm going to say no, no you can't say no to me," Kori said, grinning too.

"Come on then," Hunter said, leading Kori toward her car.

Kori was shocked when Hunter stopped at the sleek, bright blue Lexus RC F. "This is yours?" Kori asked, her eyes wide.

"Yeah," Hunter said as she opened the passenger door for Kori.

Kori got into the car, looking around the expensive interior and thinking it just didn't fit who she thought Hunter was.

When Hunter got in on the driver's side, Kori looked over at her. "You got rid of the El Camino?" she asked, her tone somewhat sad.

"No," Hunter said, shaking her head. "I just wouldn't drive that all the way down here. This was actually my wife's..." Her look flickered as she said it.

Kori winced. "Oh, Hunter, I'm sorry...I heard about your wife..." Her voice trailed off. "I'm so sorry."

Hunter drew in a deep breath, nodding. "I got your card," she said.

Kori bit her lip. "I'm sorry if it sounded really stupid, I just…I didn't know what to say, I didn't have the words…"

"What you said was good," Hunter said, remembering the card well.

The card Kori had sent had butterflies on it—monarchs actually—even though there'd been no way for Kori to know that Heather had loved them. The inside the card had said, "Strength doesn't come from what you can do. It comes from overcoming the things you once thought you couldn't." Kori had hand-written, "My thoughts are with you and your family, Hunter, please know that if you need anything all you need to do is ask."

At the time, Hunter had been far too deep in her grief to take in anything. She'd read the card later and had felt warmed by Kori's words, even though she'd never dream of reaching out to her. Kori had her life, and her spouse, while Hunter had just lost hers, and she just couldn't see past anything at that point. Still, it had felt good to know that Kori still cared in some small way.

***

Things between Kori and Hunter were different after Tom's visit. Kori had held off on telling Hunter about her feelings, sensing that Hunter was pulling away from her now. Two months after Tom had visited, Kori received an offer for a post in the Southern Region in San Bernardino. Hunter had told her she should take it but Kori had refused, throwing the letter away. They'd had an argument about it and Hunter had taken off, staying at her cottage for three days until Kori had finally come to talk to her.

They'd made up, but there was still a distance between them, and it bothered Kori no end.

Then Tom had gotten into a car accident in Los Angeles, and Kori had flown home to take care of him. He'd been in critical condition. Hunter received a couple of phone calls from Kori, and then the calls had just stopped. The next time Hunter heard anything about Kori Stanton it was that she'd accepted a position in the San Bernardino office. Hunter figured Kori had rediscovered her love for her husband while taking care of him and that was that.

Twenty-two years later, Hunter knew that Kori was still married to Tom. It said everything Hunter needed to know.

Hunter started the car, looking over at Kori. "Where do you want to eat?"

"They were talking about that Olive Garden..." Kori said, grinning. "Or is that too close to too many vegetables for you?" she asked, remembering how much Hunter had detested vegetables.

"I might survive," Hunter said, grinning as she began the short drive to the local restaurant.

"So what do you think of this Fiscal stuff?" Kori asked, glancing over at Hunter as she drove.

She took in the rings, the watch, and the bracelet, noticing as she did that Hunter still wore her wedding band. Hunter had never been much for jewelry, so it was a definite change for her. It had astounded Kori to hear that Hunter had had a wife. She'd only heard it when it had been announced that Hunter Briggs's wife had passed away due to cancer.

"I think that Fiscal is going to fuck us royally," Hunter said, sounding exactly like she had twenty years before.

Kori laughed, nodding. "Yeah, me too," she said, rolling her eyes.

"I just can't believe they can force us to abandon our processes and take on their ridiculous bullshit..." Hunter said, shaking her head.

"Yeah," Kori said, sighing. "I'm beginning to understand why Pim retired," she said, referring to the previous Director of Cal Fire.

"Congrats by the way," Hunter said, grinning.

"Uh-huh..." Kori said, narrowing her eyes at Hunter.

"What?" Hunter asked, a grin tugging at her lips.

"Don't 'what' me, Hunter Briggs!" Kori exclaimed. "I know that Midnight Chevalier had to have offered it to you first."

"Why do you say that?" Hunter asked, her look inscrutable.

"Because you're the best chief Cal Fire's ever had, that's why," Kori said, her tone sure.

Hunter looked over at Kori, her look once again unreadable. "Oh, I dunno, I'd say you did a damned good job with Southern Region," she said.

"I was never as good as you, Hunter, never," Kori said, shaking her head.

"That's where you're wrong, Kor," Hunter said, warming Kori's heart immediately with the shortened version of her name.

"She offered it to you first, didn't she?" Kori asked again.

Hunter pursed her lips, then shrugged. "I'm not executive material, Kor, you know that."

"Well, I hope that's not true," Kori said.

"What do you mean?" Hunter asked as she pulled into the parking lot of the Olive Garden.

Kori looked over at Hunter, biting her lip. The movement should have warned Hunter, but she was still stunned when Kori said, "Because I want to make you my Chief Deputy Director, that's why."

"You're insane!" Hunter said, not for the first time at lunch.

"I'm not!" Kori insisted. "Did I actually hear you order a salad?" she asked then.

"Yeah, yeah, don't change the subject," Hunter said, giving her a foul look.

"You've never met a vegetable you didn't abhor, Hunter," Kori said, grinning.

Hunter shook her head. "I learned a thing or two, okay? Jesus..." she said, rolling her eyes.

***

"You do realize that those are sprayed with pesticides, right?" the attractive blonde said to her.

Hunter was standing in Fort Bragg Safeway, in the produce aisle. She was picking up stuff to take back to the fire camp before she headed back over Highway 20 for the week.

"Not too worried about it," Hunter said, grinning.

"It's very unhealthy for you," the young woman said then, "organic is better."

"Yeah, and...a buck more a pound, I'll take my chances on the cheap stuff. It ain't for me anyway," Hunter said, rolling her eyes as she turned to leave the area.

"You're buying tomatoes sprayed with pesticides for someone else?" the woman asked, raising an eyebrow at Hunter. *"Do you hate them and want then to die?"*

"Some days," Hunter said, smiling brightly as she walked away.

Two days later, Hunter encountered the same blonde in Mendocino. Hunter was sitting on the outside balcony of one of her favorite restaurants, smoking. No one else was out on the balcony, which was the way Hunter liked it. The blonde was shown to a table nearby. She immediately looked over at Hunter.

"Smoking is bad for you," she told her.

Hunter looked back at the woman from behind the sunglasses she wore, quirking a grin.

"I'll take my chances," she said.

"You say that a lot," the woman commented drily.

"I'm a big risk taker," Hunter said, her lips curled in a sardonic grin.

"The carcinogens alone will kill you," the blonde insisted.

"Sweetheart," Hunter said impatiently, *"I eat smoke for a living, so I'm not too worried about this shit."* She held up the cigarette in her hand.

"You eat smoke for a living?" the blonde asked, her tone dubious.

Hunter nodded, smiling up at the waitress as she brought her meal. "Thanks Kim."

"Any time, honey," Kim said, winking at Hunter.

As the waitress walked away, Hunter canted her head to watch. When she happened to glance up, she could see the blonde giving her a pointed look. Hunter read disapproval in the woman's eyes and grinned unrepentantly.

"You do realize that the beef in that hamburger is actually organic, right?" the woman asked then, giving her a wry look.

Hunter looked down at her hamburger and shrugged. "I couldn't care less if I tried." She picked up the burger and took a bite.

"In the case of beef, it means that the cows were treated humanely."

Hunter grinned. "Like read a bedtime story every night and tucked in?"

For the first time the blonde actually laughed softly. Hunter couldn't deny that she was beautiful, and very definitely her type, but she also guessed the woman wasn't gay—just a pain in the ass hippie.

"That's what I like about this restaurant, everything they do is organic," the blonde said.

"Again, don't really care..." Hunter said, letting her voice trail off.

"So what did you mean by you eat smoke for a living?"

"I'm a firefighter," Hunter said simply.

"Oh..." the woman said, her voice trailing off as she nodded, looking impressed suddenly. "That's a very noble profession."

"It ain't all that..." Hunter said, wondering if this woman was likely let her eat her burger in peace.

"It's very impressive," the woman said, moving to stand. "May I?" she queried as she gestured to the empty chair at Hunter's table.

Hunter did her best not to sigh out loud, but she was sure it was in her voice when she said, "Okay..."

The woman sat down in the chair, smiling almost shyly suddenly. The waitress came out a moment later to take the woman's order. Kim's eyes reflected surprise at seeing the woman sitting with Hunter. The woman ordered a beet salad and a glass of wine.

Hunter did her best not to roll her eyes at the order; she could see Kim was doing the same.

"I'm Heather," the blonde said then, extending her hand to Hunter.

"Hunter," Hunter replied, taking Heather's hand and shaking it loosely.

"I moved here from Los Angeles a month ago," Heather told her.

"That explains a lot," Hunter said with a nod as she took another bite of her burger.

"Where are you from?" Heather asked pointedly.

"Fort Bragg," Hunter replied, with a grin, "born and raised."

"That explains a lot," Heather replied, her green eyes sparkling with humor.

"Aw, I see what you did there," Hunter said, putting her tongue to her teeth humorously.

"I'm clever like that," Heather said, widening her eyes slightly.

***

"Why in the hell would you want me as your CDD?" Hunter asked Kori, picking at the salad she'd ordered with her lunch.

Kori was still trying to get over seeing Hunter eating greens. She shook her head, trying to pay attention to the conversation. Hunter caught the shake of Kori's head, and her obvious disconcert with her eating a salad, she couldn't help but grin.

"I wasn't stroking your ego when I said you're the best Region Chief Cal Fire has, Hunter," Kori said in answer to her question. "You've always been the best at this…that's why Midnight offered you the Directorship." She looked at Hunter, her eyes searching her face. "Why did you really turn it down?"

Hunter set her fork down, sitting back, her look flickering as she shook her head.

"I couldn't..." she said simply, her look pained. "I wasn't ready, not that I think I ever would be, but..." She shook her head again, her eyes glazing with tears as she looked away. "It was too soon."

Kori felt tears sting the backs of her eyes. Seeing Hunter so affected, so obviously in pain, it brought everything back. All those feelings she thought she'd put away came rushing to the surface, making her breathless from it suddenly. Kori bit her lip to keep from gasping at the pain of her heart twisting in near agony. Seeing Hunter so emotional about someone else hurt much more than Kori had realized it would. She'd heard a few things about the year before when Heather Briggs had died, but she'd never known what to believe. What she heard about the coroner and two paramedics watching Hunter collapse when the coroner had pronounced Heather dead seemed highly feasible at that point.

"I'm sorry, excuse me," Hunter said, standing and walking away from the table.

***

Their first official date was at Heather's apartment, a fairly large studio in the middle of town.

"I'm an artist," Heather explained to Hunter as she showed her the apartment and the covered canvases at the far end.

Hunter took in the bright colors and varied textures on the canvases. Reaching her hand out, she glanced at Heather. "Is it okay if I touch it?"

Heather smiled brightly, nodding. She blinked a couple of times, like she couldn't believe that Hunter wanted to do that.

Hunter slid her finger over the canvas, touching the rough texture, then next to it a smooth surface, like glass. Then bumps like a burlap, and finally a texture like soft fur. Heather could see Hunter's eyes scanning the painting as she touched it, like she was trying to identify each aspect. She held her breath, waiting to see what Hunter would say, if anything.

When Hunter's silver eyes looked at her again, Heather waited, feeling her insides almost vibrating. It was how she always felt when someone looked at her work, like she would live or die according to whether or not they understood it.

"The colors..." Hunter said, her voice a low breathy sound, like she was being cautious about what she said and how she said it. "It's like the colors are the textures...the blue here," she said, touching the smoothness, "it's cold...like ice or like glass...and this color...what is this color?" Hunter asked looking at Heather and pointing to the reddish, rough hue.

"Cadmium," Heather said, an excited lilt to her voice.

"It reminds me of stone, like the red rock down south...in Clearlake Oaks..."

"I was inspired by Red Rock Canyon in Nevada..." Heather said, nodding excitedly.

"Yeah," Hunter agreed. "And this, what color is this?" she asked, putting her finger to the burlap texture.

"It's umber," Heather said.

"It feels like old burlap, like it should smell like ropes and sawdust..." Hunter said, her silver eyes sparkling as she looked at the painting again. "And this?"

87

"Yellow ochre," Heather said, her blue eyes staring at Hunter, her hands almost trembling with the desire to touch this woman that obviously got her work, her inspiration, her life…

Unaware of Heather's utter abandon at the moment, Hunter looked back at the color that was soft like fur. "It's like a kitten…or a tiger cub…the color is warm…like you can feel the heat of a living thing under it…" she breathed, and her silver eyes went back to Heather. "How do you make it do that?" she asked, amazed.

Heather shook her head, biting her trembling lower lip. "I don't…but you get it, don't you? You feel it."

Hunter's eyes searched hers, then she blinked a couple of times like she was coming out of a trance, looking back at the painting again, nodding slowly.

"Yeah…yeah I guess I do," Hunter said, unaware of how happy she'd just made Heather.

It took everything Heather had to keep from throwing herself into Hunter's arms in her excitement.

Dinner after that was entertaining. Heather found that Hunter was not a big fan of vegetables.

"Just try one," Heather said, offering a Brussels sprout on her fork.

"No," Hunter said, shaking her head, "sorry, but…no."

"But they're good for you!" Heather exclaimed.

Hunter grinned, nodding. "So my mother has been telling me for years."

"I'll bet she got you to eat vegetables," Heather said, crossing her arms in front of her chest.

"You'd lose that bet, babe," Hunter said, grinning.

"So you were a recalcitrant brat even then?" Heather asked.

Hunter canted her head, with a grin. "Recalcitrant brat?" She repeated with an amused tone in her voice. "I kinda like that," she said with a smile.

"Figures!" Heather said, rolling her eyes.

Later, as Heather picked up the dishes and took them to the sink, she looked over at Hunter who was sitting on her couch. Walking over, she stood looking down at her.

"What?" Hunter queried as she looked up at Heather, an expectant look in her eyes.

"I want to sleep with you," Heather said, her tone matter of fact.

Hunter stood in one smooth movement, her eyes on Heather's. "Let's go," she said, her tone heated.

Heather put her hands up, "I want to sleep with you, but I don't want to have sex with you."

Hunter took a step back. "I'm sorry?"

"You heard me," Heather said with a challenging look, "or is that something you can't do?"

Hunter looked back at her for a long moment, shaking her head. "I'm not even sure what you're asking for at this point."

Heather put her hand to the center of Hunter's chest, looking cautiously up at her. "I want to lay with you and talk with you. Can you do that?"

Hunter's look flickered with uncertainty, but she caught the challenging look in Heather's eyes. Silver eyes narrowed at the perceived dare and she nodded.

"I can do anything, babe," she said then, her tone confident.

"Good," Heather said, nodding.

Half an hour later they lay on Heather's bed. Hunter wore her tank top, sports bra, and black boxer briefs. Heather wore a long blue T-shirt with the words 'What I Am Is What I Am' after an Edie Brickell and the New Bohemians song. It was what Heather was, a bohemian—not a "hippie" like Hunter liked to call her. They lay facing each other.

"So why did you want to learn to be a pilot?" Heather asked when they talked about Hunter joining the army.

"My dad was a pilot," Hunter said, her tone wistful. "He took me up in his work chopper once and I loved it so much, I was determined to become a pilot too."

Heather smiled, nodding.

"Is he proud of you, that you did it?" Heather asked.

"He doesn't even know," Hunter said, "he left when I was sixteen."

"Oh," Heather said, her eyes sad, "I'm sorry."

Hunter shrugged. "S'okay."

Heather reached up, touching Hunter's cheek. Hunter turned her head, rubbing her lips gently against Heather's hand. She moved her lips to slide along Heather's fingers, out to the fingertips and then back down, kissing softly at the skin of her thumb. A feeling of warmth spread through Heather.

"So what was this place you were at in Los Angeles?" Hunter asked, looking back down at Heather.

"It was a commune," Heather said.

"So a hippie village," Hunter said, grinning.

"No!" Heather said laughing softly. "It was just a place where people were free to be themselves without fear or judgement."

"But where you were only with a man…" Hunter added.

"Only because none of the women there were attractive to me...not like you are," Heather said, trailing her hand over Hunter's cheek, tracing her jawline.

"All evidence to the contrary," Hunter said, rolling her eyes.

"Are you familiar with Tantric practices?" Heather asked, moving her hand to Hunter's arm and tracing the lean muscle there with her fingertips.

"Uh..." Hunter stammered, shaking her head.

"It's a way of love making that lengthens the experience..." Heather said, her fingertips brushing down Hunter's forearm.

"For who?" Hunter asked. "'Cause it sounds like a guy thing..." she said, letting her voice trail off as she rolled her eyes.

"Well, ostensibly it helps men keep an erection longer, but..." Heather said, moving her hand to Hunter's thigh, her fingertips just brushing over the material of the briefs and sliding upward under the tank top, just brushing the skin above boxer's waistline. She felt Hunter's stomach contract at the contact. "I'm sure it can be applied where women are concerned too."

Hunter shuddered at the feel of Heather's fingertips on her, thinking that it was about time they got down to business.

"So your family lives here?" Heather asked then, surprising Hunter yet again.

They talked about Hunter's family for a while.

Hunter finally shook her head, grinning. "What are we doing?"

"We're talking, Hunter, it's what adults trying to start a relationship do."

Hunter nodded slowly. "Okay, see, this is where we're having the issue then..."

"What issue?" Heather asked, confused.

"I don't do relationships, Heather," Hunter said, her tone serious. "That's not me, so, maybe we should just go ahead and..." She started to get up.

"Wait!" Heather exclaimed, putting her hand out to stop Hunter from getting up. "Just talk to me..." she said, her voice softly pleading.

Hunter heard the tone and found herself weakening immediately. She lay back down with a deep sigh, this time laying on her back, staring up at the ceiling. She remembered the last woman that was able to beg her to stay and succeed. The similarity pricked at her consciousness. She wondered what the hell she was doing. Since when did she lay and talk to a hot woman?

"What were you just thinking about?" Heather asked, having seen the faraway look on Hunter's face.

Hunter narrowed her eyes. "And I really, really hate that question."

"Why?"

"Look," Hunter said, sounding exasperated, "I think we should just give up here, okay? It's obvious we are looking for completely different things. You want a relationship, and I'm looking for a short but highly satisfying sexual encounter. So I'm just going to go," Hunter said, moving to get up once again.

"Wait!" Heather exclaimed again, pressing her body along the length of Hunter's. "Please wait..." she said, moving to lay over Hunter's body.

"Heather..." Hunter began, her tone less exasperated, but certainly not holding enough interest.

Heather moved to touch her lips to Hunter's lips, sliding her hand up over Hunter's chest, brushing past sensitive nipples, causing Hunter to shudder. It was all Heather needed. She moved her lips to

Hunter's lips again, barely touching them with her, then moving to brush her lips over Hunter's cheek, moving to her ear.

"Stay with me...." she breathed into Hunter's ear, letting her lips brush Hunter's ear sensually.

She could feel Hunter's breath coming faster and moved her lips to Hunter's neck, brushing the skin there. Hunter's hand stroked her hair. Her other hand reached up to touch Heather's cheek softly, influenced by Heather's touch. They caressed each other gently, not using too much pressure. As Heather shifted, she moved her lips over Hunter's shoulder, her hair falling over Hunter's skin.

Hunter slid her hand up under the shirt Heather wore, her fingers grazing Heather's skin. Brushing upward, she skimmed the sides of Heather's breasts, tamping down on the urge to brush her thumbs over nipples that were likely hard. She sensed that Heather wanted her to take her time, and for whatever reason she wanted to do just that too. She moved her lips to Heather's neck, brushing low at the nape, placing feathered, moist kisses on the skin there.

"Hunter..." Heather sighed. "Yes...yes..." she breathed.

Heather lowered her body down Hunter's, moving her lips slowly over Hunter's arm and down to her wrist. Hunter reached up, pulling off her tank top. Her hand reached up to touch Heather's head with the lightest pressure, encouraging her to move her lips to her body.

"Please..." Hunter found herself pleading when Heather continued to brush her lips over her hand and fingers.

Heather shuddered at the sound of Hunter's plea and knew that she was getting Hunter as heated as she was herself. She moved to Hunter's stomach, taking her time to brush her lips over all exposed skin.

When Hunter couldn't take anymore, she pulled Heather up her body, her lips capturing Heather's in a hungry kiss. Hunter's hands reached down, pulling off the shirt Heather wore. Their lips parting long enough for that to take place before reconnecting. She pushed Heather's panties down moments later. Heather was writhing against her at that point and Hunter had to grit her teeth to hold onto her control. She reached up, pulling off her exercise bra and shoving her briefs off; all the while kissing Heather's lips. Then she moved Heather under her, pressing her body against the other woman's and gyrating slowly. Within moments they were both screaming in ecstasy. Hunter continued to move over her, her lips taking possession of every inch of Heather's skin, making her cry out and come again and again.

At one point, Heather asserted herself and pushed Hunter to her back, moving herself over Hunter's body, making Hunter willing to beg, plead, and promise anything to keep her there.

When they finally lay, spent and completely sated, it was five in the morning—six hours after they'd started making love. Hunter craned her neck to look at the clock on Heather's nightstand.

"What is it?" Heather asked.

"I have to be at work in two hours," Hunter told her.

"You have to work? It's Saturday!" Heather exclaimed.

"I know, but I got newbies showing up today," Hunter told her as she went to get up.

Heather pressed closer to her again.

Hunter moaned instantly. "God…don't do that…"

Heather leaned in to kiss Hunter's neck, rubbing her body against Hunter's.

"God, honey, please…I need to get back…I need to take a shower…oh…" She groaned loudly as she gave in, pulling Heather up to kiss her lips.

It was another half an hour before she was able to finally extricate herself from Heather's body. It was one of the longest workdays of Hunter's life.

***

By the time Hunter got back to the table, their food had come.

"I'm sorry," Hunter said, "sometimes…" She shook her head.

"It's okay," Kori said, her look sympathetic.

In truth, it had given Kori a chance to collect herself as well.

As they ate, Hunter looked over at Kori. "So why me?"

Kori looked back at her for a long moment. "Because you know the stuff I don't know, Hunter."

"Which is what?"

"Well, for one, the aviation piece," Kori said. "You've probably forgotten more about aviation than I've ever known."

Hunter laughed softly. "Okay, that's probably true."

Kori smiled. "Midnight has basically given me a blank check to update our air force, Hunter, I need your help with that."

Hunter's eyes widened at Kori's statement about a blank check, then she clasped her hands together in front of her, her look pointed.

"I can do that as a chief, Kor," she said simply.

"No," Kori said, shaking her head. "I'd need you on this full time, and you and I both know that as a chief you wouldn't have time for that."

Hunter's lips pressed together and twisted in a grimace, knowing Kori was right. She was busy from the minute she got to the office till the minute she went home, usually doing ten-hour days just to try to keep up.

Hunter blew her breath out, shaking her head even as she reached for the check the waitress was bringing.

"Hunter…" Kori began.

"Don't bother," Hunter said, grinning as she handed the girl her credit card with a wink.

"Still so damned gallant…" Kori said, grinning.

Hunter shrugged nonchalantly.

Back in the car, Hunter glanced over at Kori as she drove. "Midnight asked me what I thought of you being the director, you know. So you were always in her head too."

Kori smiled softly, it was just like Hunter to try to make her feel better.

"Should I ask what you said?" Kori asked.

Hunter looked over at her, furrowing her brows. "I told her you knew your shit."

Kori chuckled. "Leave it to you to cuss in front of the Governor."

Hunter laughed, nodding. "That's why I'm not director material, Kor, and why you are."

Kori drew in a deep breath, taking in the feeling of Hunter's confidence in her.

Hunter gave her a serious look. "You can do this, you know," she said then, "you do know that, don't you?"

Kori bit her lip, something she always did when she wasn't sure of herself.

"Jesus, Kor, I wasn't blowing smoke for Midnight. You know your shit, you always have."

"Not always," Kori said, shaking her head, reaching out to touch the thin white scar on Hunter's left arm.

Hunter gave her a sharp look. "You were a three-month-old probie then, Kor, that doesn't count. And you never got lost again, did you?"

"No…" Kori said, shaking her head. "But that's because you were a great teacher."

"It's because you were a great student, Kor, because you listened to everything I said, and used it. I've had a lot of probationary firefighters, babe, you were the best I ever had, because you learned fast and you never made the same mistake twice. Hell, if you'll recall you had to save my ass at one point."

Kor smiled softly, remembering that day and the terror of the possibility of losing Hunter.

In the parking lot at the building, Hunter turned to Kori, reaching out to take Kori's hand in hers.

"You can do this," she told her again, her look sincere. "I know you can."

Kori drew in a deep breath again, nodding as she blew it out. "Will you think about the Chief Deputy Director job?"

Hunter looked at her watch. "We're late," she said, grinning as she got out of the car and walked around to open Kori's for her.

"That is not an answer Hunter Desolé Briggs…" Kori said.

"Doh! Using the middle name? Dirty pool there, Director," Hunter said, pulling out a cigarette and lighting it.

When they got back to the training room, Kori appropriated the chair next to Hunter's for the remainder of the training. They had a good time creating purchase requisitions for things like new cars, jets, diamond earrings, laughing and joking the entire time. Kori remembered easily why she and Hunter had been best friends for two years: it hadn't just been the sex, it had been the fact that they got along so well. She remembered how funny Hunter was, and how much fun they'd had shopping in stores, making jokes about fashion, or makeup, or whatever caught their attention.

At one point, Kori leaned over and put her head on Hunter's shoulder for a long moment.

"I have missed you, my friend," she said softly.

Hunter put her head against Kori's for a long moment as well. "Me too, Kor, me too." she said.

Chapter 4

At the end of the day, Hunter and Kori walked out to the parking lot.

"Did I hear that you're headed to San Francisco tonight?" Kori asked as she watched Hunter light a cigarette.

"Yeah, well, to a hotel tonight but into the office in the morning. Before the afternoon session here…why?" she asked.

"Can I hitch a ride?" Kori asked.

"As a director they don't give you a car?" Hunter asked, grinning.

"I actually came with someone else, but I'd rather leave with you, if that's okay."

"Always hitchin' a ride…" Hunter muttered with a grin.

"Hey!" Kori exclaimed, swatting Hunter on the arm like she had years before.

Hunter laughed. "Yeah, I suppose I can put up with you for a little while longer…"

"Gee, thanks," Kori said, grinning, and nodding to people as they left the training.

No one had missed how the new director and the chief of the Northern Region had appeared quite close.

Twenty minutes later they were on the road heading toward San Francisco. Hunter had music on in the car; Kori noted that she still liked her classic rock.

"So are you thinking about it?" Kori asked.

"About what?" Hunter asked, her look mild.

Kori narrowed her eyes at Hunter. "Don't get smart with me, Chief…"

"Oh…now she's got the power trip going!" Hunter said with a grin. Then she grew pensive. "I'm betting you'd want me to be in San Francisco then, wouldn't you?"

"You still live in Fort Bragg, right?" Kori asked her tone diffident.

"Yeah," Hunter said, nodding. "Although I did look into selling the house recently, but I haven't decided anything yet."

Kori bit her lip, nodding, seeing the shadow that crossed Hunter's face as she talked about selling 'the house'.

"Maybe we could work out something where you only had to come down to the office for like three days a week or something…" Kori said, desperate to get Hunter's help. "I guess that would still be a helluva commute, huh?" she said, grimacing.

"Not so bad in a helicopter," Hunter said, grinning.

"I'm sorry?" Kori queried, her look astounded. "Since when do you have a helicopter?" she asked, knowing Hunter had always dreamed of owning one.

Hunter grinned. "Bought it with the profits I made on the sale of the cottage, got it for my fortieth birthday."

"Well, that's some birthday present," Kori said, grinning.

"So worth it though," Hunter said with a smirk.

"I'll bet," Kori said. "Please, please, please think about it, Hunter…" she pleaded. "I can't do all of this without you."

"Come on, there are lots of people that know what I know," Hunter said.

"Maybe, but they don't know me like you do, and I've never worked with them before. I know I can work with you and you won't bullshit me or lie to me."

Hunter grimaced, knowing what she meant by that. "I'll think about it, okay?" she said. As she did, the song on the stereo changed.

Kori looked over, seeing Hunter staring down at the stereo, her eyes widening significantly. Then she looked upward and said, "Are you fucking kidding me?" She shook her head.

As Kori watched, Hunter reached over and turned up the song on the stereo. The song was 'Because the Night' by Patti Smith.

Hunter's lips trembled as she she reached over to put on her sunglasses.

Kori listened to the words to the song. One of the verses seemed particularly painful to Hunter, and she mouthed the words as Patti Smith sang them.

As the song ended, Hunter reached over and turned the stereo back down. Looking up again, she smiled wryly.

"Dirty pool babe…dirty pool…" she said.

"I'm sorry?" Kori asked, wondering if she was watching Hunter lose her mind.

Hunter glanced over at Kori as if just remembering she was there. Her look turned contemplative as she pressed her lips together.

"You'll think I'm crazier than you already do right now."

"Try me," Kori said.

Hunter looked circumspect for a long moment, then breathed a sigh. "Remember way back when, you and I had a conversation about ghosts and all?"

"Yeah," Kori said, nodding, "and you said you didn't believe in that kind of 'shit.'"

"Yeah, well, I'm eating those words at this point," Hunter said, her look disdainful.

"What do you mean?"

"I think my wife, Heather, is communicating with me," Hunter said, shocking Kori to her very core.

Kori blinked a couple of times. She knew that Hunter had taken her wife's death hard, and she suspected that this was simply lingering grief—it had been just under a year since Heather Briggs had died.

"And why do you think that?" Kori asked, doing her best to not sound like she thought Hunter was losing it.

"Okay, I hear the 'smile and nod and back away from the crazy person' tone, Kor," Hunter said, narrowing her eyes. "If you think for a second I didn't think I was nuts, you've forgotten who I am."

Kori grinned at what Hunter said and had to agree with the second part.

"Okay, tell me," Kori said.

"Well, Heather's always had this thing for butterflies, more specifically monarch butterflies. Back in December I was having a fairly rough time of it, with Christmas and all…" Her voice trailed off as she grimaced, thinking of the wedding she'd attended Christmas night. "Anyway, one day I was talking to her…you know, just chatting…" she said, rolling her eyes, realizing that she did kind of sound like a crazy person at that point. "And suddenly there was this monarch butterfly in our bedroom. The thing is, they usually go south when it gets cold, and this was the end of December. It landed on her picture, and then it landed on my phone. Right about the time the phone lit up with an email, the one announcing your appointment to director."

Kori looked back at her, her eyes widening slightly, and Hunter could see that Kori didn't think she was crazy anymore.

"So I picked up my phone to look at the email, and the next thing I know, the butterfly is on my right shoulder, exactly where Heather used to be whenever she was reading something over my shoulder, which was pretty often."

"Oh my God, Hunter…" Kori breathed, her eyes still wide.

"I know, right?" Hunter said. "And there's been other stuff, like this damned leaflet that kept turning up for a realtor, and now this…" She gestured to the stereo. "We're talking about me thinking about the chief deputy job and that song comes on. It was Heather's all-time favorite frigging song…" Hunter said, her voice trailing off as she shook her head. "She's definitely making her opinions known."

Kori bit her lip, feeling a chill run through her. She believed everything Hunter was telling her. She knew Hunter wasn't one to make things up and was certainly far from a believer in the supernatural.

***

Heather didn't see Hunter for two weeks. She'd called the fire camp a few times, but it took that long for Hunter to finally call her back.

"I'm sorry, babe, it's been crazy here," Hunter told her. "We're ramping up for summer, and some of these companies are way behind."

"When can I see you?" Heather asked, not bothering to play coy.

"Awww," Hunter vacillated, reaching up to rub her neck.

The fact was she'd avoided contacting Heather because she knew that Heather wanted more than she was willing to give. Hunter had plenty of experience with pissed off women who didn't get what they wanted from her. It was why she'd limited her encounters to tourists for the most part. Seeing Heather had been against her better judgement, and the amazing sex had only served to put Hunter more on edge, not less. Being as sexual a creature as she was, Hunter knew that the combination of beautiful and sexy would destroy her self-control every time, the only way to avoid that was to avoid Heather.

"Hunter, tell me when I'm going to see you," Heather said, her tone stronger now.

"I don't know. I don't think it's a good idea," she said honestly.

"Why?" Heather asked, her tone tremulous.

Hunter grimaced. She always hated this part, which was why she avoided it at all costs.

"Heather you're looking for a relationship, I told you, that's not my thing. It's just better that we end this now."

"Okay," Heather said, surprising Hunter with her change in direction suddenly. "You come to my house tonight and you tell me this to my face."

"Heather…" Hunter began.

"No, that's how this is going to go, Hunter. You come tell me to my face that this is not going to work, or I swear to all that is unholy I will come down to that camp and cause a scene the likes of which

104

you've never seen..." Heather's voice trailed off ominously and Hunter found herself responding to the threat.

"Okay, okay," Hunter said. "I'll be there tonight at seven. Okay?"

"Okay," Heather answered simply.

That night Hunter arrived at Heather's apartment, having no intention of going inside. That would have worked, if Heather's door hadn't already been wide open with Heather calling to her to come in.

"Heather?" Hunter called as she walked into the apartment.

"In here," Heather replied from the bedroom.

Hunter shook her head, knowing she was already so screwed. It only got worse when she walked into Heather's bedroom to find her sitting on the bed completely naked, her long blonde hair flowing around her.

"You're killin' me..." Hunter said, feeling her body respond viscerally to the sight of Heather's naked body.

Heather moved to get off the bed, but Hunter met her halfway, crawling onto the bed, her lips capturing Heather's immediately. They made love for hours again and lay afterwards, Hunter on her back across the bed widthwise and Heather lying next to her on her side, her leg and arm thrown over Hunter possessively.

Propping herself up on her elbow, Heather reached up, touching Hunter's lips, trailing her fingers over them.

"You're wrong, you know," Heather said.

"About what?" Hunter asked.

"About me wanting a relationship," Heather said. "I can just do sex, I've done it before, why wouldn't I be able to now?"

Hunter regarded her for a long moment, then shrugged. "If you say you don't want one, then I guess you don't," Hunter said, still

105

thinking that Heather truly did, but her body didn't care about that at that point.

The next morning when Hunter went to get up to leave, Heather stopped her, using her body pressed against Hunter's.

"When am I going to see you again?" Heather asked.

"Jesus...honey..." Hunter moaned softly. "Can you just let me call you?"

"No," Heather said shaking her head, sliding her body up over Hunter's. "You tell me a day and a time right now, or I'm going to make you so late for work..." she said, lowering her head to lick Hunter's neck sensually.

"God..." Hunter groaned, her hands grasping at Heather.

"Tell me, Hunter..." Heather said into Hunter's ear, her lips brushing back and forth, her body moving rhythmically against Hunter's.

"I can't think when you're doing that!" Hunter exclaimed.

Heather grinned, widening her eyes as she stopped moving.

"Tell me, Hunter," she said again.

Hunter was breathing heavily, because her body was still begging for the release Heather's body had already promised.

"I don't know...with the season starting...oh...Jesus!" she exclaimed as Heather put her mouth over a hard nipple. "Will you please just listen...Heather...God, God, okay! Wednesday, seven o'clock? Okay?"

"Nice..." Heather said, as she moved her body against Hunter's, making both of them come fairly quickly.

As Hunter got up, having to rush to pull her clothes on, Heather watched, her blue eyes reflecting her admiration for Hunter's physique. Hunter caught Heather's look, narrowing her silver eyes at the other woman.

"Quit looking at me like that!" she exclaimed.

"Why?"

"Because I can feel the heat in your eyes from here, so knock it off. I gotta get to work…" Hunter said, shaking her head.

Heather got up and walked up to Hunter, wrapping her arms around Hunter's neck. "I can count on you to keep your word, can't I?"

Hunter looked down at her, her silver eyes narrowed slightly. "I don't say anything I don't mean, Heather," she said simply.

"Good," Heather said, leaning up to kiss Hunter's lips softly.

"You're killin' me woman…" Hunter muttered against her lips.

Hunter turned up on Wednesday night but had to leave early because a fire had started in the lower forest, near Willits. Heather hadn't had time to secure a next time.

When she didn't see Hunter for another two weeks, Heather drove to the camp. She arrived at six in the morning and promptly asked where Squad Boss Brigg's was located. The men, stunned by such a beautiful woman showing up in the camp, pointed mutely at the squad boss's cabin.

Heather walked to the cabin, opened the door and stepped inside It was still partially dark, but she saw Hunter lying in bed, one arm over her head, the other lying across her stomach. What relieved Heather the most was that no one lay with her. She'd heard all over Fort Bragg about the "Briggs's charm" and that Hunter was well known for scoring with pretty much any woman she set her sights on. The last thing Heather wanted to be was a notch on Hunter's bedpost.

Heather turned to lock the door to the cabin, then dropped her clothing, climbing onto the bed next to Hunter. She slid under the covers, snuggling against Hunter's body. She felt Hunter start awake.

"Jesus Christ!" Hunter exclaimed, jumping. "Are you trying to give me a heart attack?"

"No, but I don't seem to be able to keep your attention any other way," Heather said.

"Jesus, Heather, I'm working!" Hunter said. "And when I'm not working I'm trying to get some fucking sleep!"

"Don't you cuss at me, Hunter Briggs," Heather said, narrowing her blue eyes at Hunter.

"I'm not cussing at you, babe," Hunter said. "But I literally went to bed"— she glanced over at the clock—"three hours ago, and I hadn't slept in forty-eight hours before that."

Heather looked back at her, her look hesitant, "I'm sorry... I didn't know that."

Hunter felt bad for snapping at the woman, but exhaustion was becoming a way of life at that point. They were down four people, and people were getting sick due to exhaustion and some kind of bug going around the camp.

"I swear, baby, I'll call you, okay? I promise," Hunter said.

Heather heard the endearment and took heart from it. "Can I just lay here with you?" she asked softly.

Hunter blinked slowly but nodded—she was too tired to even try to argue with her at that point. Heather snuggled into Hunter's side, and Hunter slid her arm around the girl, too exhausted to even react to the fact that Heather was naked against her.

It was a heavy fire season throughout California. Hunter ended up working so much that she barely had time to eat and sleep, let alone see anyone. Heather did her best to stay busy, but she couldn't help but think that Hunter wasn't making a point of seeing her. She'd started losing hope of holding on to the sexy, butch firefighter that she'd set her sights on. Things got much harder the day she talked to her doctor and he told her that the reason she'd had the "flu" for a month now was because she was pregnant. The news shocked Heather so much that she had to sit down because she'd felt faint suddenly.

By the time she found out, the doctor estimated that she was about three and a half months, quite possibly four months, and past the option for an abortion if she had wanted that. Going home to her apartment, Heather curled up on her bed, crying. She had no idea what to do. She'd never believed in abortion before, but the idea of having a baby by herself terrified her. She had no one in her life at that point, besides Hunter, who didn't even want a relationship. There was going to be no way that Hunter would want her when she found out she was pregnant. Their entire relationship was based on sex, and Heather's ability to excite Hunter. There was nothing sexy about a pregnant woman.

She was still laying on her bed when her phone rang. She thought about ignoring it, but realized that if it was Hunter, it was likely she wouldn't call back. Grabbing the phone, she answered it.

"Hello?" Heather answered.

"Is this Heather McLaughlin?" aA man queried.

"Yes, this is she," Heather said.

"Ma'am, I'm the Battalion Chief at Howard Forest Station with CDF, I'm Hunter's CO. She's been hurt and her mother suggested I call you…"

"Oh my God, where is she?" Heather asked.

"She's been life-flighted to Mendocino Coastal District Hospital, ma'am."

"I'll be there, thank you!" Heather said, jumping off the bed.

She practically ran into the hospital, going straight to the nurse's station.

"Hunter Briggs, where is she?" she asked the nurse at the desk.

"I'm sorry?" the woman queried. "Who?"

"Hunter Briggs," Heather said slowly. "She's a firefighter, I was told she was hurt and brought here. Please, tell me where she is…" Heather begged.

"I'm sorry, I can't do that, unless you're family."

"Oh my God…you don't understand, please…" Heather said, shaking from head to toe with the stress of not knowing if Hunter was alive or dead, or hurt badly.

"Take a seat miss," the nurse told her.

Heather paced, crying quietly. Suddenly, she was surrounded by men in uniforms. She looked up, looking at the faces, recognizing some of them. One of the taller men walked up to her.

"You're Heather?" the man asked.

"Yes," Heather said, tears still streaming from her eyes.

"I'm Battalion Chief Mendenhall, come with me," the man said.

Heather followed the man through the doors into the ICU. At one of the doors, he turned to Heather taking her hands in his.

"Hunter was caught behind the fire line trying to save her crew, she's got severe smoke inhalation and they're fairly certain her lungs have been damaged. She's on a ventilator and they're feeding her all kinds of painkillers and antibiotics. She's not conscious, and the doctors aren't sure what's going to happen with her, but I'm damned if

110

you're going to stay out there, instead of in here with her if this is where you want to be. Okay?"

Heather threw her arms around the big man, thanking him profusely. "Her mother is on her way?" Heather asked, knowing that Hunter's mother was the most important person in the world to her.

"Yes," Chief Mendenhall said, nodding. "We've sent a car for her."

"Good, good," Heather said, nodding. "Thank you, thank you so much…" she said, tears in her eyes again.

"Get in there to see your girl," the chief said, smiling.

Heather walked into the room and saw Hunter lying on the hospital bed. She began crying again immediately, terrified that Hunter wouldn't wake up. Heather kicked off her shoes and climbed onto the bed, careful not to disturb any of the tubes or the IV in Hunter's arm. She moved to lie next to Hunter, her head near Hunter's waist. Reaching her hand out, she put it on Hunter's waist. She lay listening to the machines click and whir and watched Hunter's heartbeat on the monitor.

She was still laying there when Maggie walked into the room. Hunter had told her about the beautiful artist she'd been seeing. Maggie had missed Kori, having hoped that Hunter would settle with the girl. She'd been very surprised to meet Kori's husband and agreed with Hunter that the man been exceedingly nice. Maggie had been very surprised when Kori left and never returned. She'd secretly hoped for Kori's return for the last two years since she'd left.

Seeing Heather laying on the bed, her hand on Hunter, however, warmed Maggie's heart toward the girl. She hadn't met Heather yet, but she'd heard a great deal about the young woman. She'd been told that Heather was four years Hunter's junior, like Kori had been.

111

She'd also heard that Heather had stormed the fire camp to track Hunter down. Maggie couldn't help but admire the girl's spirit to doggedly attempt to hold onto her fireball of a daughter. Maggie had begun to worry that she'd never get her wild child daughter settled.

As she walked over to the bed, Maggie looked down at Heather. The girl was lovely and Hunter definitely had a type. Maggie gently touched Heather's shoulder. Heather started wake, turning her head and seeing the woman that had to be Hunter's mother. She smiled softly, moving to sit up and rubbing her eyes. Maggie smiled; the girl was very definitely Hunter's type, and actually reminded Maggie of Kori.

"Hi," Heather said, feeling shy suddenly, as she extended her hand to Maggie, "I'm Heather, Mrs. Briggs."

Maggie took Heather's tiny hand in hers. "You're laying here with my daughter, so you obviously care about her," Maggie said, "so you need to call me Mom."

Heather's eyes widened, like she'd just been granted permission to call the queen by her first name. "I...okay...yes, yes I care about your daughter, way more than I think she wants me to."

"That sounds like my Hunter," Maggie said, making a face.

Heather laughed softly.

"Hunter has told me very little about you, Heather. She did say you're a very talented artist though," Maggie said, "so let's sit here and get to know each other."

By the time Hunter was out of the ICU three days later, Maggie was determined that Heather was one of the best things that had ever happened to Hunter. She was going to make sure her stubborn daughter didn't lose this one too.

Hunter woke slowly, opening her eyes and feeling her lungs burning as she labored to breathe. Fuck... she thought to herself. Looking around her she saw her mother sitting in the chair next to the bed, which meant she had been seriously hurt this time. She shifted, feeling weight to her right, and when she glanced down she saw that Heather was lying on her side, her hand on resting on Hunter's hip. Hunter smiled fondly, reaching her hand down, touching Heather's hair. Heather stirred immediately, looking up at Hunter with the bluest eyes Hunter had ever seen. Those very blue eyes widened when Heather realized that Hunter was awake. She carefully moved to sit up, reaching up to touch Hunter's face, her fingertips so gentle Hunter closed her eyes at the feel of them. Hunter made a soft grunting noise.

"Shhh..." Heather whispered. "Don't try to talk, honey, your throat is still really ripped up, so you shouldn't strain it, okay?"

Hunter nodded, closing her eyes for a moment.

She felt Heather's hand in her hair, and she thought about Kori and that last time she'd been in the hospital. That brought back the familiar ache of that loss. She squeezed her eyes shut, grimacing as she felt the tears trying to come up on her. Her throat ached wildly and she grunted in pain.

"What is, babe?" Heather asked.

Hunter reached up, touching her throat, making gasping noises as the pain grew worse.

"Okay, okay, hold on, babe, hold on," Heather said, hitting the button for the nurse.

Maggie stood up, moving to the other side of the bed so she could look down at Hunter. Heather stroked Hunter's hair, talking to her and trying to keep her calm until the nurse came in.

"What is it?" the nurse asked.

"She's in pain, she needs medicine," Heather said.

"I'll have to talk to the doctor..." the nurse said.

"Get her meds now, she should still have been on them, so someone wasn't paying attention to their job. Get them now!" Heather said, with much more force than Hunter would have ever believed her capable of.

Maggie and Hunter exchanged a wide-eyed look, and Maggie grinned.

Thinking quickly, Heather grabbed her scarf. Dumping the ice from the drink she'd had into it, she set that against Hunter's throat. The cold instantly soothed the fire in Hunter's throat and she breathed a sigh of relief, her hand reaching up to touch Heather's hand gratefully.

"Okay, honey...okay..." Heather said. "Just relax, okay? We've got you."

Two days later, Hunter was sitting up and able to talk, although the doctor had cautioned her not to overdo it. She was still on heavy duty painkillers and antibiotics—the doctors were trying to ensure that Hunter didn't get any secondary infections. Her lungs had been damaged, but the doctors were confident that she could work her way back. She'd been told that she'd need to rest for at least a month without overexerting herself.

The four probationary firefighters Hunter had been rescuing when she'd been hurt had come to see her, thanking her profusely and telling Heather how brave their squad boss was. Heather had smiled warmly, her eyes on Hunter as they talked. After they had left, Heather climbed back onto the bed, where she'd spent most of her time at the hospital. Her excuse was that it left the chair for "Mom"

114

to sit in. Hunter had noted that her mother and Heather had gotten fairly chummy while she'd been unconscious.

"I always figured you were good at your job," Heather told Hunter, sitting facing her on the bed. "But that," she said, pointing toward the door the probationary firefighters had left through, "proved how very brave you are too." Her eyes shone brightly. She bit her lip then, her eyes searching Hunter's. "I need to tell you something," she said, hesitantly.

"What?" Hunter asked, her voice husky from disuse.

Heather laid her hand on Hunter's cheek, her eyes looking directly into Hunter's. "I love you, Hunter Briggs," she said, her voice soft.

Hunter looked back at her for a long moment, her silver eyes searching Heather's face.

"You don't have to say anything," Heather said when Hunter didn't respond right away. "I know you don't want me to love you, but I'm sorry, the fact is, that I do. So you just need to get used to that."

"I do, huh?" Hunter asked, not sounding too put out by that thought.

"Yep," Heather said, grinning. "Oh, and I'm telling you right now, you are not going back to that cabin of yours at the camp when you're released from here."

"I'm not?" Hunter asked, raising an eyebrow at Heather.

"No, ma'am, you are not. The doctor said you need a healthy environment, that cabin is far from that. You will be coming back to my apartment with me."

"I do have my own place..." Hunter said.

Heather narrowed her eyes at Hunter. "Do not start with me, Hunter Briggs, or I swear I will call your mother."

Hunter's lips curled into a grin, her silver eyes glittering with subdued laughter.

It took another month, but Hunter was finally feeling normal. One afternoon she found Heather out on the small porch of her apartment. Heather was stretching and Hunter couldn't miss the slight rounding of her belly. Hunter stood leaning against the door, waiting for Heather to turn around.

"Oh!" Heather exclaimed, surprised by Hunter standing where she was. "You scared me!"

Hunter nodded, her eyes looking into Heather's. "You forget something?" she asked.

"What?" Heather asked, confused by Hunter's question.

Hunter simply looked back at her, then lowered her eyes to Heather's stomach.

Heather pressed her lips together, shaking her head. "I was going to tell you, but I wanted you to be fully better first."

Hunter nodded, her look serious.

"I found out the day that you were hurt," Heather said, feeling sick suddenly. "I...I promise you that I wasn't hiding it from you."

"Okay," Hunter said, nodding, "so what are you planning to do?"

Heather looked back at Hunter, trying to discern what she was thinking, but Hunter's look was completely unreadable. Heather took a deep breath, blowing it out as tears gathered in her eyes. She'd been dreading this moment, because she was sure this was when Hunter was going to leave.

"I'm sorry," Heather said, tears sliding down her cheeks. "I didn't, I just...I'm sorry..." she said again, unable to think of the right thing to say.

116

She looked over at Hunter, afraid of what she would say. Hunter pushed off of the doorjamb, stepped forward, and reached out to slide her hand behind Heather's neck, pulling her to her, kissing her lips. Hunter pulled back, looking down at Heather.

"I love you," Hunter said, "and I want you to marry me."

"What?" Heather asked, not believing she'd heard Hunter correctly.

"I want us to be a family," Hunter told her, putting her hand on Heather's belly, her eyes looking down into Heather's.

"Oh my God...Hunter...oh my God..." Heather wrapped her arms around Hunter, hugging her close and kissing her lips over and over.

They were married a month later, on the bluffs above the ocean in Mendocino.

***

Kori and Hunter were both silent for a while. A few songs came on the stereo, and then one started that had Hunter grinning again.

"What?" Kori asked, a grin curling her lips too.

Hunter gestured to the display that said the name of the song, 'Peace Train.'

"I take it that's one of hers?" Kori asked, amusement in her voice.

Hunter gave her a deadpan look. "Does that sound like I song I'd listen to?"

Kori laughed out loud, shaking her head. "Not really, no."

Hunter shook her head. "My little hippie…" she said, her voice soft. Her silver eyes were visible now she'd removed the sunglasses, and they took on a faraway look.

"She was a hippie?" Kori asked, surprised. Hunter had accused her of being a hippie a couple of times simply because she loved nature.

Hunter chuckled, nodding her head. "She tried to tell me she was a bohemian girl," she said with a wistful smile. "I told her that was just code for hippie."

Kori laughed, nodding. "It sounds like it. But is she the one that got you to eat vegetables?"

Hunter grinned. "The first time we met she was harassing me about my greens."

"And that worked?" Kori asked, smiling.

"She annoyed the shit out of me," Hunter said, still smiling, "she was telling me that the tomatoes I was buying for the camp were sprayed with pesticides, blah, blah, blah…"

"Oh lord, wrong tact to take with you!" Kori said.

"Tell me about it!" Hunter said. "Then the next time I meet her she's telling me how cigarettes will kill me, something about carcinogens or something…I told her I ate smoke for a living."

Kori grinned, easily able to imagine Hunter saying something like that to someone who was harassing her about her smoking. Firefighters, by and large, always referred to themselves as 'smoke eaters,' so telling one that smoked that it was bad for them was a moot point.

"Well, obviously you got past that," Kori said, smiling and doing her best to keep the ache out of her voice. It was obvious that Hunter had adored her wife, and it was painful to see.

Whatever Hunter was about to say was interrupted by the ring of her phone. Kori saw the picture on the display of the phone that said "Sam," with a picture of a beautiful blue-eyed blonde woman. Kori felt jealous instantly, more so when she saw the smile cross Hunter's lips. Then Hunter answered the call.

"Hi," she said, smiling.

"Mom?" came the query from Sam.

"Hey, baby, what's up?" Hunter asked, even as Kori's head snapped around to look at her in shock. Hunter didn't notice.

"Are you in the car?" Samantha asked.

"Yeah," Hunter said, "headed toward San Francisco now, why? What's wrong?"

"Nothing, Mom, nothing, but you need to see this place…" Samantha said, her voice trailing off in obvious awe.

Hunter rolled her eyes, shaking her head. "Let me guess…"

Samantha started laughing immediately. "You got it!"

"I'm never getting the hippie out of you, am I?" Hunter asked, even as she smiled fondly.

"Probably not, Mom got it tucked in there pretty tight," Samantha said, chuckling.

"She cheated, she programmed you from inside," Hunter said, narrowing her eyes, still grinning all the same.

"You had seventeen years to work on it," Samantha said smiling at her end of the line.

"And still so hippie…" Hunter said, grinning.

"Seriously, Mom, you need to see this place…the art-work…it's so beautiful." Samantha breathed, her voice sounding so much like Heather at that moment, it caught Hunter right in the heart.

119

Kori saw the wince and tears appear instantly in Hunter's eyes even as she turned her head to hide it. Kori could see she was breathing heavily and gritting her teeth with the effort not to cry.

"Mom?" Samantha queried worriedly.

"I'm here," Hunter said, her voice breaking slightly.

"Are you okay?" Samantha asked softly.

Hunter pressed her lips together as a fresh wave of pain crashed through her.

"Yeah," Hunter said, even as a tear slid down her cheek, "you just sound so much like her sometimes."

"I do?" Samantha asked, sounding so pleased by that thought.

"Yeah, especially when you're talking about your art," she said, smiling. "So did you look into campus dorms?" she asked then, doing her best to sound normal again.

"Yeah, I did, but Mom they're so expensive…"

"Don't worry about it, we'll handle it," Hunter said.

"Living off campus is way cheaper…"

"Nope," Hunter said, shaking her head.

"But Mom," Samantha began.

"No, Samantha."

"Just hear me out!" Samantha exclaimed.

Hunter narrowed her eyes at the phone but didn't respond.

"I met this girl here and she said that her and these other two girls are getting an apartment off campus, and that would only be like a quarter of the rent."

"No," Hunter said again.

"Mom!" Samantha exclaimed sharply.

"Samantha Renee Briggs do not raise your voice to me," Hunter said, her tone all chief at that moment.

"I'm sorry, I'm sorry," Samantha said, sounding like she truly was, "I just...I don't want to break you on college, Mom, okay?"

"Baby girl, your mother and I started saving for college for you when you born. Trust me, we've got it covered and then some, okay?"

"Okay," Samantha said. "So when can you get here?"

Hunter glanced at the clock on the dashboard. "Probably another hour or so," she said, glancing over at Kori, seeing the odd look on her face.

"Okay, I'll see you then," Samantha said.

"Hang out in the library or something," Hunter said, "don't be wandering around off campus, okay?"

Samantha sighed mightily. "Fine," she said then muttered, "I'll just stay ten forever..."

"Quit that," Hunter said, grinning. "I love you."

"I love you too, Mom," Samantha said.

"I'll see you in a bit," Hunter said.

"Okay."

Hunter hung up a moment later. There was silence in the car for a moment and then Kori said: "I'm sorry, 'Mom'?"

Hunter laughed, running her hand through her hair. "I guess you hadn't heard that part, huh?"

"That you had a kid?" Kori asked, looking at Hunter like she was insane. "No, I'd never heard that part."

Hunter grinned. "Yeah, Heather was pregnant with Sam when I met her, little did either of us know at the time."

"Wow," Kori said, her eyes wide. "I...I never pictured you with a kid...Ever."

121

Hunter gave a short laugh. "Yeah, you and me both," she said, "but I fell in love with Heather before I knew about the baby, Sam just made us a family."

Kori looked over at Hunter and felt her heart twist again. So much was different, so much could have been different, the ramifications were washing over her in waves.

***

Hunter crawled into bed next Heather, sliding her hand over Heather's very swollen belly and leaning in to kiss her softly on the cheek. Heather stirred immediately, opening her eyes.

"Hi honey," Hunter said, smiling.

"Hi," Heather replied, smiling tiredly, "you're home now?"

"Yep, off until after the baby is born," Hunter told her, sliding her arm under Heather's neck, and nuzzling the side of her head with her lips. "How are you feeling?"

"Like a house," Heather said.

"One or two stories?" Hunter asked with a grin.

Heather gave her an open-mouthed stare, but started to laugh, shaking her head. "That is a helluva thing to say to a pregnant woman, Hunter Briggs."

"I'm sorry, Mrs. Briggs," Hunter said, delighting in the sound of it, "but you are far from the size of a house and I love you."

"Much smarter," Heather said, winking up at her, "and you're really enjoying that Mrs. Briggs thing far too much, you know…"

Hunter chuckled. "Yeah, probably," she agreed. "You know, this baby is about to be born and you still haven't decided on a name for her."

"Well, I had a name for her, but you hated it," Heather said, giving her a foul look.

"That's cause I'm not letting you saddle the kid with a name like Sunshine or Flower!" Hunter said. "I'd never get the hippie out of her then."

"They're nature names, there's nothing wrong with that." Heather pouted.

"Oh, don't give me that look," Hunter told her rolling her eyes. "What's wrong with something normal like Sam or—"

"Sam?" Heather repeated. "For a girl?"

"Samantha?" Hunter said.

Heather looked considering for a moment. "I like that..." she said, sounding surprised. "But what about a middle name?"

"I don't know..." Hunter said, thinking quickly. "What about Renee?"

"Samantha Renee McLa—"

"Briggs," Hunter inserted.

"She gets your name too?" Heather asked, her tone wondrous.

"You said she's ours," Hunter said.

Heather smiled softly. "She is ours."

"Then she gets my name too," Hunter said.

Heather was still amazed that she and Hunter were actually married. One minute she'd been sure she was going to lose Hunter, and the next minute they were getting married. It had been three months since then, but Heather still couldn't believe it. They'd moved into Hunter's cottage on the coast of Fort Bragg. Heather had learned that Hunter's family had been in Fort Bragg for many generations and that they owned a lot of properties. Hunter had been left the cottage she lived in by her maternal great-grandfather and she was in line for a lot of other properties—she was one of the favorites of Briggs family favorites.

Heather was ever astounded by Hunter's family. The only person who'd ever had a problem with her being gay, her father, had left—everyone else had always been supportive of Hunter. They'd made a fairly intimidating large group when they arrived in force at their wedding, but it had quickly become evident that they loved anyone who loved Hunter.

As they lay together, Heather stroked Hunter's left arm that rested over her upper abdomen, just above her belly. She slid her finger over the thin scar there.

"What's this from?" Heather asked, having thought it before, but never asked.

Hunter grinned. "That's from my bear hunting days…"

Heather glanced sharply at Hunter. "You hunted bears?" she asked, her voice aghast.

Hunter chuckled. "No," she said, smiling, "but I did play tag with one once, when I had to rescue a co-worker during a storm, and this was my medal." She held her arm up.

"Co-worker?" Heather repeated.

"Uh-huh," Hunter said, already seeing a different light in Heather's eyes.

"Would this be Kori?" Heather asked.

At the wedding she'd heard a name a couple of times when people hadn't thought that she was around. Instead of asking Hunter, which she'd been afraid would irritate her, she'd asked Maggie about the name.

"Kori was a woman Hunter worked with about four years ago, Hunter had to rescue her early on, and they became…close."

It was all Maggie would say about the matter, but Heather knew beyond a shadow of a doubt that "close" had meant that they'd been intimate.

Hunter's eyes narrowed slightly. "Who told you about Kori?" she asked, keeping her tone even.

Heather looked back at Hunter, hearing her tone and not sure if she should say anything else, but she wanted to know and that meant she was going to need to ask questions.

"I actually heard her name a couple of times at our wedding. One of your uncles mentioned her, and so did your grandmother."

Hunter considered this—she wasn't pleased. Then she looked Heather directly in the eyes.

"What do you want to know?" she asked.

"Were you and she a couple?"

Hunter looked pensive for a long moment. Finally, she nodded slowly. "I guess we were, to a lot of people's way of thinking."

"What does that mean?" Heather asked, not wanting to assume anything.

"I considered us friends with benefits," Hunter said.

"And what did Kori consider you two?" Heather asked, knowing that Hunter always saw things her way, but it wasn't always the way everyone else saw them.

"Couldn't tell ya," Hunter said, shaking her head. "What I can tell you is that she left here one day, promising to come back and never did. So…" she said, her tone rushed and her look serious as she shrugged.

Heather's eyes widened at not only what Hunter said, but by the way she'd said it. It was apparent that Kori had been important to Hunter and something had happened to mess that up.

"You never saw her again?" Heather asked.

"No," Hunter said. "But I heard she took a job in the San Bernardino unit, so she still works for CDF. I'm sure I'll see her at some point."

"So you didn't ask her what happened?" Heather asked.

Hunter shrugged. "Why?"

Heather looked back at her for a long moment; she saw the closed look on Hunter's face and, not wanting to irritate her, she backed off. She never, however, forgot the conversation, or the way Hunter looked when she'd mentioned Kori's name.

Two mornings later, Heather woke to the feeling of Hunter's lips on her neck. They were both lying on their sides, Hunter behind her, one arm under her neck, the other lying over her torso. Heather sighed at the feel of Hunter's lips, her hand reaching up to touch Hunter's arm even as she turned her head to kiss the arm under her neck. She expected that to be the end of it, but gasped loudly when Hunter's right arm bent, so that her hand could brush over Heather's breast. The sex between them hadn't become less heated, even if it had reduced as Heather had become uncomfortable in her advanced pregnancy.

Hunter's lips traveled over her neck, kissing, sucking, and nibbling as her hand stroked nipples that were becoming harder by the moment. Heather reached behind her, sliding her hand over Hunter's hip and pulling her body closer, then sliding her hand over Hunter's ass clad in her usual boxer briefs. Her nails skimmed over the material. She heard Hunter's low moan in her ear and it caused her to shudder. Desire ripped through Heather's body as she felt her heart skip a beat. She grasped at Hunter, moaning softly, then crying out as Hunter's other hand joined the first in caressing hard nipples.

Within moments, Heather was crying out in her orgasm, her hand grasping at Hunter's body behind her as she did.

She could hear Hunter's breath in her ear and it was ragged, so she knew that Hunter was excited. Without turning over, she slid her hand up the boxer briefs, and then down inside the waistband, touching Hunter and feeling the wetness there. It never failed to thrill her to feel Hunter's excitement. Knowing that she turned this woman on made her hot every time. Hunter reached for her, sliding her hand between Heather's legs, coming against Heather's hand minutes later.

They lay together, breathless, afterwards and both fell asleep again.

"Hunter?" Heather queried a couple of hours later.

"Mmm?" Hunter mumbled as she woke slowly.

"Honey, I'm having contractions," Heather said.

"What!" Hunter exclaimed, instantly awake as she sat up and turned to look at Heather. "How far apart?"

"About two minutes apart right now and getting stronger," Heather said, extremely calm at that point.

Hunter moved to get up, pulling her clothes on.

"What are you doing?" Heather asked, an amused smile on her lips. "I'm still having this baby right here."

"I know, I know," Hunter said, nodding as she pulled her shirt on, "but I'm damned if I'm going to deliver this baby naked. I'm going to be dressed as appropriate for such an occasion."

Heather laughed at the look on her wife's face.

"Okay, babe," Heather said, her tone placating.

"Don't okay babe me, woman," Hunter said, giving her a foul look. "I'm still not completely comfortable with this, I've only

delivered one other baby and it wasn't mine, so I'm more than a little nervous."

"You will do fine, honey, I trust you," Heather said.

"You say that now…" Hunter said, letting her voice trail off, as she moved to touch Heather's knees. "I need to see if you're dilated."

"Okay," Heather said, her eyes on Hunter's.

Two hours later, Hunter was coaching Heather and the baby's head was crowning.

"One more push babe…that's it…" Hunter said, keeping her voice calm and cool. "Easy…got her!"

Samantha Renee was born at 12:43 p.m. and weighed seven pounds. Hunter immediately put the baby on Heather's chest, covering them both with a heavy blanket to keep them warm. She took care the rest of the process, then joined her wife on the bed with their daughter.

"She's so beautiful…" Hunter said, leaning down to kiss the baby, then kissing Heather. "Thank you…" she said, her tone full of the wonder.

One night, four months after Samantha was born, Heather woke to note that Hunter hadn't come to bed, even though she'd gotten home from work a couple of hours before. Heather got up, put her bathrobe on, and walked down the hallway towards the living room. She could hear music playing and realized quickly that it was rock music. Heather stood watching Hunter from a relatively hidden spot in the kitchen.

Hunter was sitting in her favorite recliner, her feet up. She still had her uniform on, although her dark blue shirt was open, exposing *the white tee underneath. Samantha was lying in her arms staring adoringly up at Hunter.*

"So what do you think?" Hunter was asking Samantha. "Are you thinking you like Bon Jovi better than Def Leppard?"

Samantha gurgled, smiling at Hunter.

"Okay, I see..." Hunter said nodding. "So where do you stand on Queensrÿche? I mean, Geoff Tate's voice is pretty awesome, you have to admit..."

Samantha waved her little fist in the air, and Hunter nodded seriously. "Okay, so I'm taking that as a 'rock on mom' gesture..." she said. "Let's give some good old-fashioned Boston a try." She reached over and changed the song on the CD player.

Heather walked into the room then, smiling at Hunter. Hunter looked up, seeing Heather walking in and smiling warmly.

"Jig's up, Sam, Mom's up now," Hunter said, winking at Heather. "Now we're going to be switching to either her hippie stuff or that snorefest stuff."

"The snorefest stuff is classical music, Hunter Briggs," Heather said, with her hands on her hips. Her smile spoiled the effect.

"Doesn't make it less boring, babe," Hunter said, even as she gestured for Heather to kiss her.

Heather leaned down, meeting Hunter's lips, and then leaned down further to kiss Samantha's little face.

"Babe, it's after midnight," Heather said, moving to sit down on the floor in front of Hunter, putting her head against Hunter's leg.

"I know," Hunter said, grinning, "but she was awake, and I didn't want to wake you. I gave her a bottle and now she's really awake. So I thought I'd start educating her on good music."

"Versus my hippie stuff?" Heather asked, her look pointed.

Hunter grinned unrepentantly. Heather shook her head at her wife, loving the woman to distraction. In the end, Heather ended up sitting with them until Hunter and Samantha fell asleep. Heather got up, covering both her wife and her daughter with a blanket, and kissed each of them gently on the head. She then lay down on the couch, surveying her little family and loving it.

***

Hunter noticed that Kori had gone silent. She wasn't sure what it meant, but didn't figure it was her place to ask too many questions. After a few minutes Kori looked over at Hunter.

"How old is Samantha?" she asked, hoping her voice sounded normal.

"She's seventeen," Hunter said. "She graduates high school in May."

Kori nodded, calculating that Hunter must have met Heather somewhere around two years after she'd left Fort Bragg. She did her best to take to heart in the fact that Hunter hadn't immediately moved on and fallen in love, when Kori hadn't been able to get her to love her.

Hunter glanced over at Kori, still not understanding her sudden quiet mood.

"You okay?" Hunter asked.

Kori took a deep breath, blowing it out slowly and nodding. "Just kind of trying to catch up at this point."

"Catch up?" Hunter repeated, her tone even, but her look quizzical.

Kori caught Hunter's look and smiled tightly. "You know, on everything that happened after I left…" she said, knowing that she sounded ridiculous.

Hunter's eyes narrowed slightly, as she looked out the windshield.

"Well, what happened is that you never came back, so…" she said. Her tone was conversational, but her look indicated that she fully blamed Kori for that occurrence.

Kori nodded quickly, knowing that it had been her choice not to go back, and that she'd made that decision without discussing it with Hunter…or anyone for that matter.

"I guess maybe an explanation is in order," Kori began.

Hunter shook her head. "No," she said simply.

"What?" Kori asked, having readied herself to tell Hunter the whole thing.

"I don't need, or even want, an explanation, Kor," Hunter said. "You stayed with your husband. It made perfect sense."

Kori gave a short humorless laugh. "I guessed that's how you'd see it," she said, her tone sad.

Hunter heard the tone but steeled herself against it. She hadn't made the choice, Kori had, and it had had lasting ramifications.

***

"So you'll see her," Heather continued doggedly.

"I'm guessing so," Hunter said as she put items into her bag.

Heather didn't look happy about that at all. Samantha chose that moment to come running into the bedroom, climbing up on the bed.

"Where ya goin?" Samantha asked, smiling up at Hunter.

"To Los Angeles," Hunter answered.

131

"Where's that?" Samantha asked, her four-year-old curiosity always on overdrive.

"It's about five hundred and fifty miles south of here," Hunter told Samantha. "Do you know which way is south?"

Samantha pointed down triumphantly.

"You got it!" Hunter said, grinning at her daughter.

"Yay!" Samantha exclaimed clapping her hands.

"Sweetie, can you go play in the living room? Mommies are talking right now," Heather said patiently.

"Okay!" Samantha agreed, hopping off the bed and running out of the room.

Hunter grinned, shaking her head. "I wish I still had that much energy."

"You've got enough," Heather said, but it clearly wasn't a compliment.

Hunter looked back at her, surprised by her attitude.

"Jesus Christ, Heather, what do you think I'm going to do? Go to Los Angeles, find Kori, and fuck her?"

"Do not cuss at me, Hunter," Heather said.

"Then stop being so friggin' irrational," Hunter said.

"I don't think I'm being irrational," Heather said, her blue eyes flashing. "I think that this woman is seriously unfinished business for you and I'm worried about how you're going to react when you see her again."

"Oh for fuck's sake…" Hunter said.

"Hunter!" Heather exclaimed, never liking it when Hunter cussed.

Hunter shook her head, her look closing off suddenly. "I'm not doing this shit with you Heather, I'm not..." she said, her voice trailing off as she zipped up her duffel. "I have a flight to catch."

With that, she picked up her duffel bag and strode out of the room. Heather heard her saying goodbye to Samantha. She staunchly refused to go running after Hunter. She felt her heart sink when she heard the front door close and the El Camino start with a roar.

In Los Angeles, Hunter had seen Kori from across the training room they were in and had purposely not made eye contact. It had definitely hurt to see her again. Hunter noted that she still wore her wedding ring, so she knew Kori was still married to Tom. It was all she needed to see.

It was the longest week of Heather's life. Hunter didn't call and Heather forced herself not to call either. As far as she was concerned, if Hunter was going to cheat on her with Kori no amount of phone calls was going to change that.

On Friday night when Hunter got back, Heather waited on the front porch, her hair blowing in the wind. As Hunter walked up the steps of the porch, she could see that Heather had been crying. Without a word, she took Heather into her arms, kissing her lips, then hugging her. She led her into their house and took her straight to their bedroom. It was late, so Samantha was asleep. Hunter had taken her time that night making love to her wife for hours.

Just before they fell into a sated sleep around four in the morning, Hunter moved her lips to Heather's ear.

"I love you, Heather Briggs. I love you and no one else will ever mean to me what you do. You need to know that."

133

Heather nodded, closing her eyes and clinging to those words. They never fought about Kori again.

***

"Can you just drop me at the Bart Station?" Kori asked quietly a few minutes later after a long silence, and as Hunter neared the exit for UC Berkley. "It's right on the way to the college."

"Sure," Hunter said, nodding, taking the exit.

"So you'll be in the office tomorrow morning?" Kori asked, her tone reserved now, as Hunter pulled into the Bart station parking lot.

"Yeah," Hunter said.

"Okay."

"Kor…" Hunter began as she parked, not sure how get beyond the past at that point.

"It's okay, Hunter," Kori said. "I get that I fucked up where you're concerned. I've always gotten that," she said, her voice sounding tearful. "Have a good night," she said as she got out of the car.

Hunter watched as Kori strode into the Bart station, seeing her reach up to wipe at her eyes. Hunter sat thinking about what Kori had said, her mind in turmoil. Shaking her head, she put the car in gear and headed over to UC Berkley to meet Samantha.

That evening at dinner with Samantha, Hunter told her daughter about what Kori had asked her to do.

"So she wants you to be her deputy director?" Samantha asked, taking a drink of her soda and looking back at Hunter.

"Yeah," Hunter said, nodding.

134

"And what does that mean? You'd be like a higher executive than you are now?"

"I'd basically be second in command," Hunter said.

"Wow…" Samantha said, widening her eyes. "I thought you were pretty high up there already though."

"It's not about the title, Sam," Hunter said.

"What's it about then?" Samantha asked, her tone serious.

Hunter realized that Samantha had heard Heather and she discussing matters like this before, and that Samantha was now taking on the role that Heather usually did. She was asking open-ended questions to let Hunter work things out in her head. Hunter smiled fondly at her daughter.

"What?" Samantha asked, seeing Hunter's proud smile.

"I'm just so proud of the woman you're becoming," Hunter told her.

"Why do you say that?" Samantha asked, even as she lit up at the praise.

"Because you are becoming such a good person—understanding, empathetic. It's a really good thing, babe," Hunter said, "you're a lot like your mother."

"And you," Samantha added, her look pointed.

"Maybe a little like me," Hunter said with a grin. "Only the tiny little good parts though."

"There is nothing but good parts about you, Mom," Samantha said, her eyes narrowed.

"Yes dear," Hunter said, grinning.

"Anyway, tell me what this job would be about," Samantha said.

"Well, Kori's got carte blanche for updating our air force and that's the part she wants me to do."

"Aren't you always complaining about how far behind your aircraft are technology-wise?" Samantha asked, taking a bite of her salad.

"You heard that, huh?" Hunter said, grinning.

"Since I was about ten and knew what 'POS' meant," Samantha said, grinning.

Hunter laughed, her laugh so engaging that a number of women in the restaurant turned to look at her. Hunter didn't notice, but her daughter did. They were at Fable in the Castro; the place was trendy, but nice enough. Samantha had insisted on going to the Castro, the predominantly gay section of San Francisco, having never seen it before.

"I love it," she'd commented as they were driving around to find a parking space. "It's like they put a rainbow flag on anything that stood still long enough."

Samantha had noticed that her mother got a lot of looks from women. Hunter had a very definite look to her that attracted attention. She was definitely butch, with her dark hair, tanned, lean face and light silver eyes…Hunter's build was a very lean, but strong. And her style of dress had a cool edge to it, thanks to Heather's careful ministrations.

On this particular evening, Hunter wore well-fitted jeans with her black combat boots, and a vintage Pink Floyd 'Dark Side of the Moon' shirt with the prism and rainbow cover art. Over it, she wore a purple button-up shirt, completely open, and a black jacket with the sleeves pushed up to her elbows, the purple shirt sleeves folded over so they showed. She wore her thick banded black watch and black leather band on the other arm. Even Samantha knew that her mother was hot to other lesbians, but Hunter didn't pay any attention.

"Do you even notice all the women looking at you?" Samantha asked her mother.

Hunter looked around them, seeing a number of women looking in their direction. A few of them actually winked at her. Hunter's look was blasé as she glanced back at her daughter.

"Do you see anyone in here that's anywhere near as beautiful as your mother was?" Hunter asked her daughter.

"Kori Stanton is as beautiful as Mom was," Samantha said.

"And married to the same man for twenty-two years," Hunter said.

"But obviously into you for a while," Samantha countered.

"Key words there, baby girl, 'for a while,'" Hunter said. "Now, can we change the subject?"

"Are you not going to take the job because you two were a thing?"

"If I decide not to take the job, it won't have anything to do with my previous relationship with her, Samantha. Business is business. What we do is too serious to let emotional bullshit get in the way."

Samantha's eyes widened at what Hunter said, but then she nodded, respecting her mother's words.

"She is really pretty, though…" Samantha said, smiling.

"She is definitely beautiful," Hunter agreed, "and she hasn't changed one damned bit in twenty years. How do girls do that?"

"Magic," Samantha said, grinning.

Chapter 5

Hunter walked into the San Francisco Cal Fire offices carrying her coffee. Samantha walked in behind her, noting that a lot of people knew her mother. She received a lot of nods, and people saying "Good morning, Chief" or simply "Chief" respectfully. Hunter smiled and nodded to everyone. She led Samantha to her office.

"So you get two of these?" Samantha asked, having been to her mother's office in the Fort Bragg Cal Fire offices a number of times.

"Yeah," Hunter said, grinning, "I guess I do."

"Lucky!" Samantha exclaimed. "When I'm a full-fledged adult, I want to be important enough to have two offices too."

"Uh-huh," Hunter said, as she pushed her door open. Samantha stepped inside and saw how many pictures there were of her and her mother.

"Wow…" Samantha said, looking around the office. "Nice."

Hunter grinned, doing her best to keep her eyes off all the pictures she had of her girls. She'd forgotten how many there were of Heather—she hadn't been to this office since before Heather had gotten sick.

***

Hunter had gotten home from work and found that Heather was still in bed. She checked on Samantha in her room who was working away on her homework.

"Can we talk about how much algebra sucks?" Samantha commented to Hunter.

"We can, but it won't suck any less," Hunter said, grinning as she leaned on the doorjamb to Samantha's room.

"I'm beginning to hate high school..." Samantha said.

"Give it time, you'll hate it less," Hunter told her. "Have you seen mom tonight?"

"She got home from the doctor's and went back to bed, she's still feeling crappy."

"Okay, I'll go check on her, then start some dinner," Hunter said.

She walked into their bedroom to see Heather lying on the bed. Kicking off her boots, Hunter walked over to the bed and sat down, reaching out to touch Heather's cheek. Heather stirred immediately. Hunter leaned over, kissing Heather's lips.

"How you feeling, babe?" she asked.

Heather moved to sit up, her movements pained, and Hunter went to help her. Heather leaned heavily against her. She'd been sick for weeks, and the doctors hadn't been helpful at all, telling Heather that it was cold and flu season and just to drink fluids and rest.

"Did the doctors say anything new?" Hunter asked.

Heather shook her head. "They gave me a prescription for that Tamiflu stuff."

"Are you kidding me?" Hunter asked. "Do they really think you've had the damned flu this long?"

"Don't cuss," Heather said softly.

"Oh, I'm gonna cuss, I'm gonna cuss at those morons who can't seem to get it through their thick skulls that you need more than their ridiculous prescriptions. We're going back in there tomorrow, and they're going to do something for you, and that's final."

"We really need to work on those venting skills of yours, babe..." Heather said smiling softly.

"I know, I'm such a slow burn kinda girl..." Hunter said, her silver eyes narrowing.

"Uh-huh," Heather said, grinning up at Hunter.

Hunter hugged Heather to her. "I'm going to go make some dinner, okay?" she said. "You rest, I'll bring it in to you."

"Babe, you worked all day..." Heather said, feeling bad that she wasn't helping more.

"I'm an exec now, you know we don't work," Hunter said, winking at her.

Heather chuckled, shaking her head. "You always work hard, Hunter Briggs, I know that, don't try to fool me."

"Yes, ma'am," Hunter said, smiling. "Rest."

"Okay," Heather said, her stomach already bothering her again.

That night Heather did her best to eat some of the soup Hunter made, but her stomach wasn't having it. The doctor's office said she'd lost twenty pounds in the last three weeks. She didn't tell Hunter that—she didn't want to worry her.

True to her statement, Hunter took Heather back to the doctor the next day. She insisted that they do more tests and find out what the Hell was wrong with her wife.

"Ms. Briggs, you don't understand," the doctor began, his tone placating.

"Do a fucking CT Scan on her stomach," Hunter growled, gritting her teeth. "Or I swear to God I will beat the crap of someone in this hospital, and it's probably going to be you."

"We don't do CT Scans for the flu, Ms. Briggs," the doctor said sharply.

"She doesn't have the flu, you fucking idiot!" Hunter snapped, as she stood up, leaning over the man's desk. "She's been sick for three weeks! Do the fucking scan or I'll find someone who will!"

A week later, Hunter was wishing she'd never forced the issue. The scan had been done, and they'd found a tumor on Heather pancreas. It had been biopsied. Heather was in the hospital, because she'd spiked a fever during the procedure. The doctor had pulled Hunter into his office and had given her the news that Heather had stage four pancreatic cancer.

She stared blankly at the man, blinking slowly. "What?" she asked, sure that she'd heard him wrong—she had to have heard him wrong.

"I'm sorry, Ms. Briggs, there is very little we can do. We will certainly try chemotherapy and surgery to remove the tumor, but the prognosis is not good. I'm so very sorry."

Hunter shook her head numbly, feeling her whole world start to crash around her. What was that roaring in her ears?

"Ms. Briggs?" the doctor queried, looking at her expectantly.

"What?" Hunter asked, doing her best to focus though she wanted to throw up.

"I asked if you want me to tell her."

"No," Hunter said, shaking her head, "no, I'll talk to her."

The doctor nodded. "I'm very sorry," he told Hunter again.

Hunter nodded and stood.

Outside the doctor's office, she leaned against the wall, breathing heavily as she tried to gather her courage. Pushing off the wall, she walked down the hall to where Heather was. Taking a deep breath, she walked into the room. Heather was awake but groggy.

"Hi honey," Hunter said, smiling down at her.

"Hi," Heather said, smiling softly.

Hunter leaned down, kissing her lips softly. Pulling back she looked down at her, praying her devastation wasn't showing in her eyes.

"Rest honey, okay? Just rest, I'll take you home tomorrow."

"Okay," Heather said, smiling again.

Hunter stayed with her until she was asleep. Then she got up slowly and walked toward the exit. Outside, she got into her El Camino, forcing herself to hold it together on the short drive home. When she got home, she got out and walked around to the back of the house. She couldn't go inside, not yet. Sitting down outside on one of the patio chairs, she stared, unseeing, out at the blackness of the night sea. Winter was on its way in and the wind was freezing. Hunter didn't notice.

As she sat there, it started hitting her. She started to shake and her breathing became erratic. Thinking about having to watch Heather die made her lose it. The tears started slowly at first and then became an unstoppable torrent. She had the impression of her body shaking violently, but her mind was spiraling around and around one thought: she was going to lose the woman she loved. Nothing would stop it, nothing would keep her there.

The shaking became so violent, she started throwing up, unable to calm herself enough to stop it. The noise alerted Samantha to her being out there.

"Mom?" Samantha queried, her voice terrified.

"God, honey, please…don't come out here…please…" Hunter said, shaking her head, her breathing coming in short gasps. "Please honey…just go inside, please?"

When Samantha didn't move, Hunter yelled at her to go. Samantha jumped and ran inside. She immediately went to the phone and called her grandmother.

Maggie answered the phone.

"Grandma?" Samantha queried her voice tearful.

"Honey! What is it?" Maggie asked, knowing that Heather had been sick and worried that something might have happened.

"Please come, Grandma, please… It's Mom…please come!" Samantha begged.

"Okay, honey, I'll be there as fast as I can. Just hold on," Maggie said, grabbing her keys and running out of the house.

Hunter had told her that Heather had a mass the doctor's wanted to look at, but she hadn't heard the results. Now she was worried she knew.

Ten minutes later, Maggie stepped out onto the back porch of the house and saw her daughter falling apart. Hunter had her knees up to her chest, her arms wrapped around them, her head down on her knees. She was shaking from head to toe and her breath was coming in short, ragged gasps. Walking over to her, Maggie reached out, touching her head.

When Hunter lifted her head, Maggie felt her heart lurch. She'd never seen her daughter so completely devastated before. Tears streamed down her face, she looked so lost.

"Hunter, what's happening?" Maggie asked, fear in her voice.

"She's dying, Mom…" Hunter said, her voice broken.

"What?" Maggie said, tears in her eyes instantly.

Hunter shook her head, as if trying to deny it to herself at this point.

"She's dying…I'm going to lose her…" she said, still shaking her head. A fresh wave of tears began again. "I can't do this! I can't do this…" Hunter said, sounding panicked suddenly. "Mom I can't…I can't…." Her breathing was labored and rasping.

Maggie moved to take her daughter into her arms, holding her as she cried. Closing her eyes, Maggie knew she was hearing the sound of her daughter coming completely undone. The idea that Heather would die was beyond comprehension, it just wasn't possible.

When Hunter finally quieted, Maggie reached over to grab one of the chairs on the patio. Pulling it over, she sat down, looking at her daughter.

"Tell me what they said," Maggie said.

Hunter's face took on a faraway look, like she was trying to distance herself from what she was about to say.

"The doctor said it's pancreatic cancer. That by the time she showed symptoms it was probably already too late…"

Maggie winced, they'd lost a few family members to cancer. It was a horrible and devastating way to watch someone die.

"What can they do for her?" Maggie asked softly.

"Surgery, chemo, the usual bullshit that'll just make her sick…" Hunter said, her lips trembling as she blinked slowly. She started to shake her head again. "I don't think I can handle this, Mom…I don't think I can do it. I can't lose her, I can't…"

Then she was crying again, her body wracked by sobs. Maggie cried with her.

Finally, she sat back, looking down at her daughter. "Hunter, you need to listen to me now," Maggie said, her voice strong.

Hunter lifted her head, looking at her mother.

"I know that this is the hardest thing you've ever had to go through," Maggie said gently, "but I am here to tell you that you can do this, and you need to do this. You need to be here for your wife and daughter. And you need to be strong for them. Do you understand me?"

Hunter closed her eyes slowly, blowing her breath out shakily. Her lips trembled, but she finally nodded.

"This is going to the be the most important thing you've ever done, Hunter," Maggie told her. "You are going to have to go through hell with her, but if you're not there for her every step of the way, you will hate yourself later."

Hunter winced at what her mother was saying, but she also knew that it was true.

"You need to give Heather all of your love and support, and you're going to need to be there for Samantha too. This is not going to be easy, honey," Maggie said, tears in her eyes again, "but I know you can do this for them. I know it." She put her head to Hunter's. "You are so strong, baby, you have always been so strong. Now you need to be strong for them."

Hunter nodded again, blowing her breath out.

"We need to tell Samantha," Maggie said. "I think she already knows that it's bad, but she needs to know what's happening exactly."

Hunter started hyperventilating. "Oh God…I don't know…" she said, faced with the prospect of telling her daughter that her mother was dying.

Maggie took both of Hunter's hands in hers. "She needs to know, Hunter, this is not something you can shield her from. You and Heather have never lied to that child, now is not the time to start."

Again Hunter breathed out a loud whoosh of air, then she nodded, looking at her mother. "Will you stay with me to tell her?"

"Of course," Maggie said, nodding.

Hunter put her hand to her forehead, noticing that it was shaking like a leaf in a stiff wind. "Just give me a sec, okay?"

"Okay," Maggie said, moving to stand. She was already very worried about Hunter's state of mind.

She'd truly never seen her daughter this way, so unsure of herself and so terrified. Maggie knew that Hunter was strong, but she wasn't sure that this experience wouldn't completely shatter her either. She knew she'd need to keep an eye on Hunter throughout this time.

Maggie went inside, seeing Samantha sitting in Hunter's chair. The girl already looked haunted, Maggie thought. Maggie moved to sit in the chair and reached out to take the girl's hand.

"Is she okay?" Samantha asked softly, nodding her head toward the patio.

"She will be, honey," Maggie said.

Samantha nodded, blinking a couple of times. She knew something was happening, and she knew it was bad. She'd never seen Hunter so completely out of control before, it had terrified her. Hunter was always the strong one, her mom was the one that always cried and got upset about things—even things as simple as the ASPCA commercials on TV. Heather cried about that kind of thing, Hunter just shook her head and handed her wife the checkbook to write a big donation. This was different and Samantha knew that it was going to be devastating.

Maggie and Samantha sat quietly, holding hands and waiting for Hunter to come inside.

It was twenty minutes before Hunter could bring herself to walk into the house. The warmth of the house as compared to the freezing wind outside struck her so physically she felt like she could faint. She put her hand out on the doorjamb, closing her eyes slowly and taking slow breaths until the dizzy feeling passed.

She walked inside, looking over at her mother and daughter sitting in the living room. Walking over to the kitchen, Hunter took down a bottle of tequila and took a big swig, letting the warmth spread through her. Finally, she put the bottle away and walked into the living room. She knelt in front of where Samantha sat, reaching up and taking both of Samantha's hands in hers.

"It's Mom, isn't it?" Samantha said, unable to bear the uncertainty any longer.

Hunter nodded, tears shining in her eyes again. "Yeah, baby, it's Mom. She's really sick."

Samantha grimaced, tears forming in her eyes as she nodded, her lips trembling as she did.

"I'm sorry, baby…" Hunter said, shaking her head, "but it's cancer, and there isn't a lot they can do."

Samantha began to cry openly then, and Hunter felt her heart break a little bit more. She hugged her daughter to her, holding her as she sobbed. Tears were flowing down her cheeks too, but she held onto her control, not allowing her devastation to overwhelm her again. Her mother was right, she needed to be strong for Samantha right now. This wasn't about her grief, it was about making sure Samantha was okay.

"Can…I…" Samantha began, but hesitated.

"Can you what, baby?" Hunter asked gently.

"What kind of cancer?" Samantha asked softly.

"Pancreatic," Hunter said.

"She's going to die?" Samantha asked, her voice a barely audible whisper.

Hunter closed her eyes, but nodded, her lips trembling again as a tear slipped down her cheek. "Yeah, honey, she's going to die."

Samantha nodded, crying again. Hunter held her to her chest, looking over at her mother who was crying at that point too. Maggie nodded to her to tell her she was doing good.

"But we're going to take care of her, okay?" Hunter told Samantha. "You and me, we're going to take care of her and make sure she has everything she needs…"

"Is she going to have to do chemo?" Samantha asked.

"Yeah," Hunter said, "it sounds like it, but it's going to be up to her."

"Up to her?" Samantha asked.

Hunter nodded. "This is her decision, baby, it's her life, and we're going to respect whatever she wants to do."

Samantha looked like she wanted to argue, but she saw the look in her mother's eyes and knew that it wouldn't do any good. She hoped that her mother would decide on chemo, it would give them more time. Samantha knew about cancer, enough of Hunter's family members had dealt with it over the years that it was a familiar enemy.

That night, Maggie went home and Hunter and Samantha went to bed. During the course of the night, Samantha crawled into bed next to Hunter, like she had many years before as a child. Hunter held her daughter, knowing they were about to face the worst days of their lives. She just hoped she could get Samantha through it. She *wasn't sure she'd make it out the other side, but she was going to get their daughter through it, no matter what it took.*

The next day she picked Heather up from the hospital, bringing her home and settling her in bed. Heather could tell Hunter was on edge, she wouldn't settle down—constantly getting up and adjusting things.

"Hunter?" Heather queried when Hunter had gotten up for the third time in ten minutes.

"What? You need something?" Hunter asked, turning to look at her.

"Yes, I need you to tell me what's wrong," Heather said. "Did the doctor tell you the results? Is it bad?" she asked, her voice gentling on the last part.

Hunter had to use every ounce of strength she had to keep from crawling onto the bed and crying herself sick in her wife's arms. Instead, she moved to sit on the bed.

She nodded in answer to Heather's question. "Yes, he gave me the results, and…yes, it's bad."

Heather drew in a sharp breath, tears in her eyes instantly. She felt cold suddenly, all the way to her core. There was an ache in her stomach—a cold knot of terror.

"Tell me," she said softly.

Hunter relayed everything the doctor had told her. By the time she was done they were both crying. As she had the night before, Hunter forced herself to stay in control of her grief. She knew she couldn't let Heather see how scared she was, it would only shake Heather more.

When Heather quieted, Hunter moved to sit against the headboard of the bed, holding Heather against her.

"I'm going to take a leave of absence," Hunter said, "and I'm going to be with you through everything, okay?"

Heather nodded, too overwhelmed at that moment to protest anything.

"Does Sam know?" Heather asked softly.

"Yes," Hunter said, "I told her last night."

Heather breathed a sigh of relief. "Thank you," she whispered, "I can't begin to imagine how hard that was for you, but I know I couldn't do it."

Hunter nodded, having known that too.

"We're going to take care of you, babe," Hunter said. "We're going to do everything we can to take care of you."

"Until the end," Heather said, her voice breaking on the last word.

Hunter had to fight back the lump in her throat that was threatening to suffocate her with her pain. "Through everything."

Heather nodded again, still feeling devastated. Thoughts ran through her mind that she'd never get to watch Samantha get married, have kids or even...graduate?

That thought had Heather asking, "How long?"

Hunter blew her breath out. "They don't know," she said, "they can do surgery to remove the tumor, and then there's chemo..." Her voice trailed off, knowing that Heather knew all about those things.

"But it all just delays the inevitable," Heather said. She was shattered.

Hunter nodded, unable to reply because her throat was constricting.

Heather looked up at Hunter and saw the devastation in her eyes. Reaching up, she put her hand to Hunter's cheek.

150

"I want to do whatever it takes to fight this off for as long as we can," Heather said. "I want to stay with you and Sam for as long as possible."

Hunter couldn't hold back her tears any longer, as relief flooded her veins. She'd been terrified that Heather would refuse to do anything to stop the inevitable, and Hunter wasn't sure she could argue with her to make her try anything. She pulled Heather into her arms, partially out of sheer gratitude, and also to comfort her again. She held her as they both cried.

***

Hunter and Samantha were each working on their own thing in Hunter's office when there was a knock on Hunter's office door.

"Come!" Hunter called, still typing on the report she was working on.

"Hey, I—oh, hi," Kori began as she walked into Hunter's office, then she saw the beautiful blonde girl sitting at Hunter's small conference table.

She knew it had to be Samantha, Hunter's daughter. She took in the honey blonde hair and big beautiful blue eyes that were now staring at her with interest.

Hunter looked over and saw Kori and Samantha looking at each other. She couldn't help but grin at the situation. Ex-girlfriend meets daughter of deceased wife.

Hunter turned, looking at Kori. "Kor, this is Samantha," she said, gesturing to her daughter, "Samantha, this is Koriander Stanton, the Cal Fire Director."

As she'd been taught, Samantha stood up, walked over to Kori, and extended her hand to the other woman, nodding respectfully.

"It's nice to meet you, ma'am," Samantha said.

"It's nice to meet you too, Samantha," Kori said, looking over at Hunter who smiled fondly. "Wow, this is more respect than I get from most of my firefighters. I may need to hire you after you finish at Berkley," she said with a wink.

"Not sure how much demand Cal Fire would have for an art major, ma'am," Samantha said with a smile, "but it would be great to work with my mom."

"Oh, art major, huh?" Kori asked, surprised.

"My birth mother was an artist," Samantha said, a flicker of sadness crossing her face. "A good one, right Mom?" she said, looking over at Hunter again.

"A very good one," Hunter said, smiling.

Another shock to Kori's system, Hunter had married not only a hippie, but an artist? Would the wonders never cease?

"So what's up?" Hunter asked, seeing the odd look on Kori's face and not understanding it.

"Well, I was hoping I could catch a ride to Sacramento with you…" she said, her voice trailing off as she rolled her eyes heavenward innocently.

Hunter chuckled. "I swear that a company car comes with that director's hat," she said, with a shake of her head.

"You know I hate to drive," Kori said.

"I know you hated to drive Highway 20…" Hunter qualified.

"Well, I hated to drive period, but especially 20," Kori said with a grimace.

Hunter chuckled.

"Please? 'Cause my only other option is driving with Healy and…" Kori's voice trailed off as Hunter started to laugh.

"And he'll force you to listen to classical music all the way there and want to have an entire discussion about the existential merits of Beethoven versus Bach or some shit."

"Yeah, so save me? Again?" Kori asked, her look pleading.

Hunter blew her breath out in an exaggerated sigh. "Fine! Always having to save your ass... I swear..."

"Thank you!" Kori beamed. Then she looked over at Samantha. "She did save my life once, you know. My favorite bear hunter," she said with a fond grin.

"I heard part of the story," Samantha said, looking over at Hunter, "but maybe you can tell me the whole thing."

"How about I take you two to dinner tonight, and I can tell you then," Kori suggested, then looked over at Hunter. "When's the last time you had a really good steak?"

"Ohhh..." Hunter groaned, looking heavenward then shaking her head. "That's just bribery there," she said, her tone sly.

Kori smiled widely. "I'm betting they still don't have a decent steak house in Fort Bragg, am I wrong?"

"You are not wrong," Samantha said, laughing and looking over at her mother.

"So you're a steak eater too?" Kori asked.

"Oh yeah," Samantha said nodding.

"Much to her mother's chagrin," Hunter said, smiling fondly at Samantha.

"Oh God, Mom would get so upset with the rare steaks..." Samantha said, her voice trailing off as she shook her head and smiling all the while.

"Was she a vegetarian?" Kori asked, looking between the two women.

153

"No," Hunter said, "but she really hated how much red meat I consumed."

"Oh boy," Kori said, grimacing, "that must have been a battle."

"A constant one," Samantha said, smiling.

"And then you turned traitor and liked red meat too," Hunter said to Samantha.

"I thought Mom would never forgive me," she said, laughing.

"She didn't talk to either of us for a week after you came out as a carnivore," Hunter said winking.

"Well, three days at least," Samantha said, laughing.

"So she was pretty serious about it, huh?" Kori asked, smiling.

Hunter rolled her eyes, nodding.

"You still look like you're maintaining your fighting weight," Kori said with a soft look on her face. "So obviously whatever she was doing was good for you. And I actually witnessed you eating a salad, so she was definitely a miracle worker."

"Uh-huh," Hunter said, giving her a warm smile, then she looked over at Samantha. "What do ya say, babe? Wanna let Kori take us to dinner?"

"I think definitely, yes," Samantha said.

"And there you have it," Hunter said nodding to Kori.

Three hours later Kori, Hunter, and Samantha left the office. Hunter dropped Samantha off at the Bart station—she was going to do some more college tours—and then she and Kori headed to Sacramento. The music in the car was playing and Hunter was singing along with whatever song was on.

As Hunter got onto the freeway that led to the Bay Bridge, Kori looked over at her.

"Hunter, I want to apologize for yesterday," Kori said softly.

Hunter glanced over at her, then shook her head. "There's nothing to apologize for."

"There is, Hunter," Kori said, "yesterday I was really having a hard time with all of this and I took that out on you. I shouldn't have."

Hunter's look flickered slightly, but then she shrugged. "It's understandable that things are gonna be a little weird between us, Kor... I mean, we kind of ended really...abruptly."

"And if you'd let me explain what happened—" Kori began, but Hunter held up her hand in a halting gesture, shaking her head. "Hunter please," Kori said, her voice beseeching, "I hate that you think that I just left and forgot about you. Please let me explain."

Hunter's lips twisted in an agonized grimace, but she nodded. "Okay, tell me," she said, her tone holding a note of worry.

Kori nodded thankfully. "When I got back to LA, I was going back and forth to the hospital a lot. Tom was in and out of consciousness and they weren't sure what was wrong...anyway, at the hospital I kept smelling this terrible smell that made me sick to my stomach every time I was there. I finally complained to one of the doctors and he looked at me like I was nuts. So I talked to one of the nurses and she gave me funny look too, but different, you know? They both told me that there was nothing abnormal smelling that would cause me to be sick, that it was obviously something going on with me. I went to my doctor, and he told me I was pregnant."

Hunter glanced over at her looking shocked. "Jesus, Kor…" she said, wincing.

Kori nodded sadly. "It must have happened when he came up to Fort Bragg…I knew I shouldn't have…but…"

"But he was your husband, Kori," Hunter said.

"But I didn't love him, and I knew that."

Hunter shook her head. "You're still with him, Kor, there must have been something there."

Kori laughed softly but it was a humorless sound.

"Yes," Kori said, nodding. "In the absence of anything else, I'm still with him, you're right."

Hunter looked over at her, her look searching. "What does that mean?"

"It means that I couldn't be with the person I wanted to be with, so I stayed with what was safe," Kori said.

"The person you wanted to be with?" Hunter asked sounding mystified.

Kori looked over at her, her look saying that Hunter knew what she meant by that.

Hunter shook her head. "You never told me. You called me twice, but you never told me."

"I didn't know before I called you, I really still thought I was coming back at that point," Kori said. She shook her head sadly. "I knew that you'd run for the hills if I showed back up pregnant with his kids."

"Kids?" Hunter asked.

"Twins," Kori said, smiling softly.

"Wow," Hunter said, amazed. Then another thought occurred. "That's why you were so shocked when you heard about Sam yesterday."

Kori gave a short laugh. "Yeah, you could say I was shocked. I really never imagined you would have a kid, and hearing that you did, so shortly after…I just thought that I'd really screwed up in my thinking."

Hunter looked over at her again, seeing the self-castigation Kori was going through.

"Don't beat yourself up too much, Kor," Hunter said, "I can't tell you how I would have reacted if you'd told me you were pregnant then." She said it honestly. "As it was, I was already freaking out about Tom…I'd built it into my head that he was an asshole, a beer guzzling, football watching, male chauvinist and that was why you were with me. But when I met him…" She shook her head. "He was such a nice, likeable guy. If you'd told me that you were pregnant and that you were leaving him and taking away his kids…" Her voice trailed off again. "I don't know that I would have been able to handle that, then."

"But you handled Heather being pregnant," Kori said.

"That's because I was two years older and wiser, plus there was no man in evidence accepting responsibility for the baby. I fell in love with Heather before I even knew she was pregnant. I held onto her when I got hurt and she told me she loved me, because I didn't want to lose her like I lost you."

Kori bit her lip at the sound of those last words. Fate was a cruel character sometimes. She'd lost Hunter and had sent her into the arms of another woman because she'd been too afraid to try and keep her.

They were both silent for a while, each lost in their own thoughts. Then Kori heard Hunter mutter, "Seriously?"

She looked over at her. Hunter was looking at the display on the stereo even as she turned up the song that was playing. It was Adele's 'Someone Like You.' The first few lines said it all, talking about having heard that the other person settled down.

Kori looked over at Hunter again. "So you think this is her?" she asked, referring to Heather.

Hunter laughed softly. "Probably," she said, "Adele isn't exactly my thing."

Another verse made Kori's heart ache painfully. It referred to how hard it was looking back and seeing all the mistakes that made the present so bittersweet. It was definitely true enough.

Kori looked over at Hunter as the song ended. "The problem is, there's no one like you, Hunter, and I guarantee you that Heather knew that too."

Hunter looked over at Kori, surprised by her statement, and not knowing what to say in response. She wasn't sure why Heather had sent that particular message, but it tugged at Hunter the rest of the day.

The training session in Sacramento was mercifully but irritatingly short.

As they climbed back into the car, Hunter grumbled, "That was three hours of my life I'll never get back."

"Right?" Kori said, shaking her head.

"But at least there's steak in the offing, right?" Hunter asked, grinning.

"Yes, ma'am, we already have a reservation and everything," Kori said, smiling.

"Awesome," Hunter said, raising her eyebrows in delight. "Oh I should warn you…" Hunter began, her voice trailed off as she widened her eyes at Kori.

"About?" Kori asked, seeing the mischievous look in Hunter's eyes and knowing it far too well.

"Well, before you have dinner with me and Sam tonight, you should know that Sam knows who you are."

Kori turned her head slightly, narrowing her eyes at Hunter, hoping Hunter wasn't saying what she thought she was saying.

"What do you mean who I am?" she asked. Hunter started to grin.

"You mean from…" Kori started to say and Hunter started to nod her head. "Oh my God, Hunter why would you tell her that!" Kori exclaimed.

"Well," Hunter said, "she could tell I was on edge when we left the house to come here and I don't lie to my daughter about anything, so…when she asked what was going on, I told her that I was going to see someone I hadn't seen in a long time."

"Okay…" Kori said, her tone leading.

"Let's just say she figured out that you weren't an old enemy," Hunter said, her lips curling into a grin again.

"Oh God…" Kori said, starting to feel a little like a teenager caught with a boy, or in this case, a girl, in her room.

"I'm only telling you because she has an insatiable curiosity and since she's seventeen, she's got no filter, so she's likely to ask you questions. I didn't want you blindsided."

159

"And you expect me not to lie to her either?" Kori asked, sounding slightly panicked.

Hunter reached across the center console touching Kori's hand. "I expect you to tell her whatever you feel comfortable telling her, even if it's that it's none of her business. Okay?"

Kori drew in a deep breath, nodding slowly.

"I'm sorry, Kor," Hunter said, "I really didn't think about how this would go if she met you."

"It's okay, I'm not ashamed of the time we spent together, Hunter, I guess I just didn't think I'd have to face someone like your teenage daughter about it."

"If it helps, she thinks you're really cute," Hunter said, smiling roguishly.

"Is she gay?" Kori asked.

"Not that I know of," Hunter said. At Kori's queried look she added, "I think she thinks you're cute for me."

"As in for you...like *for* you?" Kori asked.

Hunter chuckled, nodding.

"Wow," Kori said simply.

As Hunter expected, Samantha's questions started almost instantly. No sooner had they taken their seats at the table and given their drink orders did Samantha look over at Kori.

"So, you dated my mom?" she asked.

Kori's eyes widened slightly, but then she nodded, looking over at Hunter.

Kori was still trying to still her heart from seeing Hunter dressed the way she was in almost all black—black slacks, a slate-grey collared shirt, and a black jacket that was cut perfectly for her. She'd added leather dress boots and a leather belt with a stylish brushed silver-and-black enamel buckle. At her throat she wore a black corded necklace with a dog tag shaped silver pendant, a Fleur-de-Lys relief in the center. To Kori's surprise, instead of the thick banded watch she usually wore on her wrist, Hunter wore a sleek black Movado watch. In a word, Hunter looked incredible.

Hunter looked back at Kori, smiling and rolling her eyes to say *I told you so*.

Hunter was having a bit of a hard time as well, with the way that not only Kori looked that evening, but the way she had smelled when she'd hugged Hunter when she and Samantha had entered the restaurant. Kori wore a fitted black sheath dress with four diagonal spaghetti-style straps at the top over each shoulder. She'd pulled a fitted black jacket over the top, and four-inch heels that had made her almost as tall as Hunter. A very nice expanse of toned and tanned leg was exposed, since the dress stopped at mid-thigh. Hunter couldn't believe she'd forgotten how hot Kori's legs were, or was it that they'd gotten hotter over the years?

Samantha noted the way that her mother was looking at Kori, and she'd also noted that Kori was very much checking out Hunter. She wasn't sure how she felt about that, but it had her asking questions.

"How long did you two date?" Samantha asked, looking between Hunter and Kori.

"About two years, but I wouldn't say we dated in the classic sense of the word," Kori said, her eyes straying over to Hunter again.

"We were pretty, um…casual," Hunter said, a sardonic grin on her lips.

"Friends with benefits," Samantha said.

"Right," Hunter said, nodding.

Samantha put her hands together on the table in front of her, "Were you in love with my mother?"

"Sam…" Hunter said, her tone admonishing.

"It's okay, Hunter," Kori said, looking back over at Samantha. "Yes, I was in love with her."

Samantha nodded, her look considering, then she narrowed her eyes. "Then why did you leave and never come back when you said you would?"

"Samantha Renee Briggs!" Hunter exclaimed, her tone harsh. "Kori, you don't have to answer that. Samantha, that is none of your damned business."

Samantha winced at the tone in her mother's voice, she knew she'd gone too far, but it bothered her that Kori had hurt her mother.

"I'm sorry," Samantha said, her eyes downcast.

"It's okay," Kori said, looking at Hunter and shaking her head slightly. "I'll answer you, actually. I didn't come back because I found out I was pregnant, and I didn't think your mother would want me under those circumstances."

"She married my mother when she was pregnant with me," Samantha said, as if that negated what Kori had said.

Hunter put her hand out, placing it on the table in front of her as she looked over at her daughter. "What you need to know, Sam, is that I wasn't the committing type when I was with Kori, so her assumption was fairly safe then. And you should also know," Hunter said, looking over at Kori, her eyes on her as she said the next part, "that it was losing Kori because of my being too scared to commit, that made me smart enough to grab your mom and hold on to her."

Samantha looked back at Hunter, surprised.

"So, basically it's because of Kori that you're my mom now?" Samantha asked.

Hunter smiled. "Basically, yeah."

Samantha blinked a couple of times, and then nodded. "So I guess I should thank you and stop being a pain in the ass, huh?"

Before Kori could answer there was a crash of dishes falling and breaking in the kitchen that had almost everyone in the restaurant jumping in shock. Hunter pressed her lips together, glancing up.

"Think that was Mom?" Samantha asked, grinning.

"Could have been," Hunter said, grinning too.

A waitress walked by, talking to the bus boy. "I don't know how that happened, I wasn't anywhere near that counter..." Hunter started laughing then, shaking her head.

"Destructive little sprite," Hunter said.

"Hoping she's on my side," Kori said, her eyes wide as she grinned.

Samantha looked over at Kori then, surprised that Kori seemed to know about Heather's presence. She was pleased that not only did Kori seem to know, but she also seemed to believe.

***

Hunter was lying next to Heather. She'd just been through her third round of chemo, and had been sick repeatedly until she'd fallen into an exhausted sleep. Hunter kept watch on her, wanting to make sure she was there if Heather woke up and needed something. Her hand still moved in circles on Heather's back to continue to soothe her, even though she was sure Heather was asleep. Samantha poked her head in the doorway to their bedroom.

"How's she doing?" Samantha whispered.

Hunter grimaced. "This round was rough," she said softly, "I don't know how much of this she's going to be able to take."

Samantha drew in a deep breath, her eyes shining with tears, even as she nodded. She knew that her mother was doing her best to go through chemo so she could stay with them longer. Heather had already lost a lot of weight and her hair was thinning more every day. She'd cried about it the day before, prompting Hunter to shave her head down to the lowest point on the trimmers. Heather had raged at her for a half an hour, but then given up.

"Nice hair, Mom," had been Samantha's only comment, understanding fully why Hunter had done it.

It was a couple of hours later when Heather stirred, opening her eyes and looking up at Hunter who was sitting reading a report on her iPad. Hunter looked down at her immediately.

"How are you feeling baby?" Hunter asked softly.

"Okay," Heather said, her voice weak.

Hunter reached down, smoothing her thumb over Heather's cheek gently, leaning down to kiss her lips softly.

"Do you need anything?"

Heather shook her head, her look pensive. It took her another couple of minutes however, to say, "Hunter?"

"Yeah babe?" Hunter responded.

"I think you should call Kori," she said, her tone hesitant.

164

Hunter looked shocked by the statement. "What? No," Hunter said, her tone sharper than she'd meant it to be.

"Hunter, you need to know what happened," Heather said.

"I don't need to know what happened," Hunter said, her look defensive, "why are you doing this?"

"I just think that you and Kori—"

"There is no me and Kori, Heather," Hunter interrupted angrily. "There's me and you, that's all."

"But when I'm—"

"Don't!" Hunter exclaimed sharply, tears in her eyes. "Don't do this Heather, please…" Her throat constricted painfully.

"I just want you to be happy," Heather said softly.

"I'm with you. I am happy, Heather," Hunter told her, her tone still impatient in her heartbreak.

"But I don't want you to be alone."

"Then don't leave me!" Hunter snapped, and instantly regretted it when Heather paled and her lips trembled. "Oh God, babe…God…I'm sorry…I didn't mean that," she said as she gathered Heather in her arms, hugging her gently. "I'm so sorry…I love you so much…I'm…I'm sorry."

"It's okay," Heather said against Hunter's neck, tears in her voice. "I don't want to leave you, Hunter, ever…but…there's nothing we can do about that."

"I know, but I hate it…" Hunter said, her voice trailing off as she shook her head.

"Me too," Heather said softly.

"Please stop trying to push me away, babe, okay?" Hunter asked.

"I'm not trying to push you away, Hunter, but I know that you loved her, and I want you to find love again."

"I found love, babe, I found you."

"But—" Heather began, but Hunter's on her lips silenced her.

They kissed softly for a while, until Hunter felt her getting tired again. Lying back, she cuddled Heather in her arms. She was trying to take in every moment with her, knowing that at some point she'd lose her, and would regret any moment she'd lost with her. It had been four months since the diagnosis.

They'd done surgery removing the mass, but it was spreading, and it had slammed the door on any chance of recovery. It was a matter of time, and Hunter knew they were just dragging things out. It worried her how sick Heather was getting with the chemo. She knew it went against everything Heather was to pump poison into her body to try and beat back the cancer that was killing her. Hunter was trying to decide how selfish she wanted to be with her wife's life, and it was crushing her to do it.

On this particular night, she waited for Heather to fall asleep again. She got up carefully, so as not to disturb her. Pulling on her boots and jacket, she walked down to Samantha's bedroom.

"I'm gonna go see grandma for a bit," Hunter said, her tone as light as she could make it.

Samantha looked up from her homework, and nodded, moving to stand.

"Okay, I'll go keep an eye on Mom," she said.

Hunter leaned down to kiss her daughter on the cheek. "Thank you, baby," she said, never sure if Samantha knew why she went to grandma's or not, but appreciating that she always responded instantly to Hunter's need for a break.

Outside, Hunter climbed into her El Camino and started it with a satisfying roar. She focused only on her driving as she sped down the *highway to her mother's inn. Once there, she parked on the street and walked inside. She poked her head into the kitchen, spotting her mother. Maggie turned to see Hunter in the doorway, nodding to her.*

"Go up, I'll be there soon."

Hunter went upstairs to her mother's area in the large house. Going over to the refrigerator, she pulled out a beer, opened it and drained the bottle in one long drink. She reached for another beer, moving to sit on her mother's couch and letting the first beer start to warm her insides. She hadn't eaten all day, so it worked pretty fast.

Maggie walked into the room, carrying a sandwich on a plate, knowing that Heather had gone through chemo early in the morning and that Hunter rarely ate on those days. She could see that Hunter was already two beers in. It was a bad one, then, Maggie thought to herself as she put the plate in front of Hunter's face. Hunter shook her head numbly.

"Hunter you need to eat," Maggie told her.

"She's trying to get me to call Kori," Hunter said, her level of intoxication evident.

"I don't know that it's a bad idea, Hunter," Maggie said. Seeing the sharp look she received from Hunter, she held her hand up. "She was your best friend too, Hunter Desolé, don't give me that look."

"Yeah, well, the lover part trumped that, Mom, and I can't change that now," Hunter said, moving to lay down on the couch and putting her head in her mother's lap.

Maggie reached down, stroking her head. "What did you do to yourself?" she asked, her hands touching the short spikey hair.

"Heather was upset about losing her hair. So I lost mine," Hunter said shrugging.

Maggie shook her head, astounded by her daughter's willingness to do literally anything for her wife. She was, however, extremely proud of the strong woman she'd raised in Hunter.

"I don't know how long I can let her do this, Mom…" Hunter said softly, her eyes starting to tear up. "She's so sick…it's so awful on her."

"She wanted to do this, though, right?" Maggie asked.

"Yeah, but she's doing it for us, Mom, you know she hates all that crap they're giving her."

"You and Samantha are worth it to her, Hunter," Maggie said.

Hunter shook her head sadly, her tears flowing over. "I can't watch her fade away, Mom. It's breaking my heart."

"You have to let her do what she feels that she needs to do, Hunter," Maggie said. "This is her choice."

"But if she's doing it for us…"

"Because she loves you," Maggie said.

"But what quality of life is this?" Hunter asked. "She has maybe one good day, and the rest are just a nightmare of throwing up and pain and feeling so weak…"

"But she's with you, Hunter, she's with you and Samantha and that's what she wants."

Hunter shook her head, giving in to the need to cry for everything she was losing. They were heart-wrenching, painful sobs, and Maggie did her best to soothe her as she cried. It broke Maggie's heart every time she heard her daughter fall apart this way, but she wanted her to do it there, instead of in front of Heather or Samantha. Maggie knew that it was likely the only thing that was keeping Hunter sane at that point in time.

Part of her really wished that Hunter would call Kori. Maggie knew without a doubt that Kori would be there for Hunter if she'd let the girl be, but her headstrong daughter wouldn't hear of it. Maggie didn't push it because she knew that alienating her right now would only keep Hunter from coming to her to release all her pent-up emotions. Maggie didn't want to think about what could happen if Hunter didn't have an outlet for her pain. She couldn't take that chance.

She stroked Hunter's head until she had cried herself out and slept for a while. When Hunter woke, Maggie made her eat the sandwich she'd made her—Hunter had lost a lot of weight while taking care of Heather and it worried Maggie. Hunter didn't have an ounce of extra weight on her to lose, losing anything was too much.

Hunter walked back into her house four hours after she'd left. Walking into her bedroom, she saw Samantha asleep in the chair next to the bed, her hand in her mother's. Standing in her doorway, Hunter looked at the two women who meant the most in the world to her. She was going to lose one of them and she knew that Heather would take a large chunk of her heart with her when she died. Hunter wasn't sure she'd ever recover.

Chapter 6

The weather Hunter had been worried about moved in that night. A storm of wind and rain beat at the hotel windows all night and into the morning. Kori arrived at the hotel via Uber. For the first time in the week, she wore jeans, a powder blue sweater, and a black leather and sweat jacket liner hoodie, with black leather lace up boots.

"Look at you, all butch…" Hunter said, grinning as she opened the hotel room door to Kori.

She said it, but Kori looked far from butch. Her makeup was perfect, and her long curly hair pulled back at the top with the rest flowing around her shoulders. She looked dammed good and Hunter found herself remembering more about Kori than was comfortable at that moment.

"Butch, huh?" Kori asked, unaware of the direction of Hunter's thoughts.

"Maybe only a little bit," Hunter said, winking at her. "I'm just about ready," she said, sitting down on the bed to pull on her boots. Kori looked around, seeing that one of the doors to the suite was closed.

"Samantha still asleep?" Kori asked.

"Yeah," Hunter said, grinning, "she's not a real fan of storms, so we ended up awake half the night watching movies till I could get her calm enough to sleep."

Kori smiled softly. "You're a good mother, Hunter."

Hunter grinned at Kori. "Heather always said I was the best father Samantha could have had."

"That's probably true too," Kori said, agreeing with Heather on that one. "Are you sure you're okay to drive? You aren't too tired?"

"I'm okay," Hunter said, reaching over to show Kori the coffee cup from the Starbucks down the street. "Double Espresso," she said, grinning. "I'm good…"

"Oh lord," Kori said, rolling her eyes, "I remember how much the squad boss used to hate it when you'd have too much caffeine in the morning."

"Put the fire in your ass out, Briggs!" Hunter exclaimed, in a close imitation of the squad boss's tone.

Kori laughed, nodding.

"Ah, the good old days," Hunter said, grinning almost sadly.

They got on the road a little while later. Traffic was a mess and the rain was pounding the car.

"Maybe we just forget Fiscal for the day and go back to the hotel and take a nap…" Hunter muttered.

Kori glanced over at Hunter, wondering if she realized what she'd just said—she seriously doubted it. Even so, Kori felt a shiver go through her at the very thought of lying next to Hunter again. She'd never forgotten how Hunter had made her feel; being with her had been so exciting. It was those memories that often kept her awake at night. She'd long ago stopped sleeping with

Tom. He just didn't excite her at all and she'd gotten tired of faking it for him. Part of her had hoped he'd just ask for a divorce then, but he hadn't.

When they finally made it to Sacramento, they were late. Hunter led Kori into the building, signing them both in. They had just walked into the hallway that led to the training room, when someone called out, "Briggs!"

Hunter turned and started grinning. A tall woman walked up to Hunter and hugged her. There were two other women with her: one was very butch looking with short dark hair, similar to the way Hunter's hair was cut. She was young, with gauges in her ears. The other was a blonde with long, rainbow braids hanging from under the white blonde hair. All three women were dressed casually.

"Kor," Hunter said, turning to her. "This is Gun, Sydney, and Harley," she said, gesturing to the women. "They work for OES. Guys, this is Kori Stanton, she's the new director over Cal Fire and a good friend of mine."

The woman Hunter had called Gun extended her hand to Kori, smiling. "Nice to meet you," she said, with a very definite come-on in her dark eyes.

"I'm tellin' Sable..." the woman called Sydney said, as she stepped over to extend her hand to Kori. "Hey," she said smiling.

The third woman was looking down at her phone and glanced up long enough to give Kori a quick salute with her index finger before she started tapping at the phone.

"Don't mind her," Gun said, grinning. "Harley's kind of...well, she's extremely ADHD. If you're not a computer or her girlfriend she doesn't have time for you."

172

Kori chuckled at the description.

"So what are you girls doing here?" Hunter asked.

"Trying to get a stay of execution," Sydney said, glancing over at Harley and rolling her eyes. "This Fiscal bullshit is going to murder us. We're hearing processing times are like twice as slow," she said with a grimace.

"There's an option for getting out of using the system?" Kori asked, her eyes widening with interest.

"I'll let you know," Gun said, smiling warmly, "you two should have lunch with us."

"Aww." Hunter hesitated, looking over at Kori. Kori nodded. "Okay, sounds good. We'll meet you out front at noon."

"Got it," Gun said, winking at Kori. She turned to walk back the way they'd come, taking Harley's arm and walking her backward. Harley glanced up, grinning at Hunter and turning around to fall into step with Gun and Sydney.

"Interesting…" Kori said, watching the three women go, "and you know them how?"

"Long story, and we're late," Hunter said as she turned to walk toward the training room.

When she glanced beside her and Kori wasn't there, she looked back. Walking back a couple of steps, she took Kori's hand and pulled her along toward the training room.

All Kori could think about was the warmth of Hunter's hand in hers. It took her five minutes to even be able focus on the training.

"Hunter says it's a long story how she knows you girls," Kori said when they were all settled at a table for lunch, "but I'm betting it's not that long of a story."

She narrowed her eyes at Hunter. Hunter grinned back at her as she chewed the ice from her glass, her look completely innocent—which told Kori she was far from.

"Not much of a bragger, huh, Hunter?" Gun said, grinning at her.

"I just flew the copter," Hunter said, shrugging.

"Wasn't there something about the tide coming in?" Sydney asked, her hazel eyes sparkling in amusement.

"There was definitely a tide issue," Harley said. She'd finally focused on them because Sydney had removed her phone from her hands and set it on the other side of the table.

"Yeah, and my lady lying on a rock about forty feet down," Gun said.

"Okay, wait, wait, wait!" Kori said. "Just tell me what happened."

"We were in Mendocino," Gun said.

"We?" Kori asked.

"A group of us, we were there for my wedding."

"She's married to Sable Sands," Hunter put in.

"Seriously?" Kori asked, looking at Gun.

"Yeah," Gun said, grinning.

"And you're still flirting?" Kori asked. "With a woman like that on your arm?"

"A beautiful woman's a beautiful woman, babe," Gun said, waggling her eyebrows. "It's a requirement that a beautiful woman be paid attention to, or we butches aren't doing our jobs."

Kori looked over at Hunter, who grinned, nodding. She looked at Sydney and Harley who both nodded as well.

"Oh...kay," Kori said. "Unanimous on that one. Anyway, keep going."

"So Sable's out on the...um..." Gun stammered, looking over at Hunter.

"She was out on the bluffs in Mendo, you know off of Main Street," Hunter told Kori.

"Oh, yeah," Kori said, nodding. "Go on."

Gun grinned. "Anyway, one minute she's there the next she's gone."

"The bluffs gave," Hunter told Kori, "this was in December."

"Oh yeah, those were some serious wicked storms," Kori said, remembering that she'd thought about Hunter during those storms, having seen that the coast was getting pounded.

"Yeah, Sable fell onto a rock down below, and none of us could get to her. Suddenly here comes your girl, in her helicopter. It was the most beautiful thing I'd ever seen," Gun said, smiling at Hunter. "She picked me up and lowered me down to the rock so I could get to Sable. Then she got us off that rock before the tide got us."

"I remember you taking a bit of a bath," Hunter said, grinning.

"Damned cold one too," Gun said, laughing.

"Winter on No Co, baby," Hunter said, her silver eyes sparkling.

Kori looked over at Hunter. "So you rescued Sable Sands?"

"No, her wife rescued her, I just flew the copter," Hunter said.

Gun leaned over to Kori. "She rescued both of us," she told Kori softly in her ear.

Kori turned and looked at Gun, narrowing her eyes. "Behave," she said.

Gun laughed out loud at that one, nodding her head.

"So are you in San Francisco now, Gun?" Hunter asked, remembering that Gun was being moved up there.

"Yeah, me and Syd are up here."

"And what do you do for OES?" Kori asked Gun.

"I'm the Chief Deputy Director," Gun said, sounding highly unimpressed with herself.

"Uh, Gun, you're a co-director now, remember?" Sydney said.

"Jesus, whatever…" Gun said, rolling her eyes. "I could be chief bottle washer, nobody would care less."

"So you're in charge?" Kori asked.

"Up here," Gun said.

"And you?" Kori asked looking at Sydney.

"I'm a…uh, what did they just make me?" Sydney asked, grinning.

"Assistant Chief Information Officer," Harley put in, "it's how you can afford an apartment in San Francisco."

"For her and Mia…" Gun said, grinning.

"Mia?" Kori asked.

"Her girlfriend," Harley said, smiling.

Sydney looked down, pressing her lips together, looking shy all of a sudden. Kori found it very endearing.

"She's very cute," Hunter said, winking at Sydney.

"Yeah," Sydney said, a very sweet smile on her lips.

They talked about other topics then, and Kori found that she really liked these women. Harley, when she was focused on people, had a great, ironic sense of humor. Sydney was just plain cute, and Gun, while appearing to be a major flirt, was very obviously in love with her rock star wife.

"We need to get together soon," Gun said as they finished their lunch. "I know Sable would love to see you." Gun looked over at Hunter.

Hunter nodded, grinning. "Did you two find a place in the city?"

"Oh yeah, on edge of the Castro somewhere," Gun said, grinning.

"Somewhere?" Kori asked.

"Yeah," Gun said, "I dunno, Sable's agent found it. I just drive there."

Kori laughed, nodding. "At least you can find your way home, that's important."

"When your wife has a bodyguard that's ex-IRA, trust me, you come home when you're supposed to," Gun said cheekily.

On the drive back to San Francisco that afternoon, Kori looked over at Hunter.

"Okay, I've been really good all day yesterday and again today and not bugged you," she said, grinning, "but have you thought about my job offer at all?"

Hunter grinned, wondering when she was going to get around to asking that question.

"I have," she said, her tone completely non-committal.

"Okay…" Kori said, her tone leading.

"You're really sure about this?" Hunter asked, gesturing to what she was wearing—faded jeans and a black button-up shirt, with a black biker style jacket over the top.

"Hunter, I don't care what you wear, but frankly your style has actually stepped up a bit since I knew you…I imagine that was Heather's influence."

Hunter chuckled. "You know me, put something in front of me, unless it's a dress, I'll probably wear it."

"Well, I like it, and no, I don't care if you're not a business suit kind of person, that's what I consider my job."

Hunter nodded. "Good, 'cause I really don't like suits."

"I know," Kori said, grinning, "and I promise I'll never make you wear one."

"Then I guess I'm in," Hunter said, grinning.

Kori wrapped her arms around Hunter's right arm resting on the center console. She leaned her head against Hunter's shoulder, squeezing her arm.

"Thank you!" she exclaimed happily.

"Remember you said that," Hunter told her, grinning.

***

They'd been through another round of chemo, and Heather threw up constantly. The morning after the treatment, Hunter lay holding Heather against her. She knew what she needed to do, but she wasn't sure if she would have the strength to do it. She was so lost in her thoughts that she didn't see Heather open her eyes. Heather reached up touching her cheek gently.

"Hey…" Hunter said, smiling down at her, "how are you feeling this morning?"

178

Heather swallowed convulsively, grimacing. "Still kind of yucky."

Hunter nodded. "Want to try some ginger?"

Heather smiled softly. "Look at you, all hippie and stuff…"

"Boho, remember?" Hunter said, chuckling, even as she reached for the ginger candy she'd found online that seemed to help Heather with the nausea.

Heather laughed softly as she nodded. Hunter put the candy in Heather's mouth, pulling her closer again.

"I was just lying here thinking about that first time we met," Hunter said.

"And how much I annoyed you with my hippie stuff?"

"Yeah, that," Hunter said, grinning.

Heather blinked slowly. "I just wanted an excuse to talk to you," she said, her voice gentle and soft.

"Yeah?" Hunter asked, smiling. "Why'd you want to do that?"

"Because you were so handsome, and you just had this presence…I could feel you from a mile away."

"Hmmm," Hunter murmured.

"But then you got away from me so quickly."

"Because you annoyed me," Hunter added.

Heather laughed softly again. "But then I saw you again in Mendocino and thought that fate had brought us together again."

"And you answered fate by harassing me again," Hunter said, smiling.

"I didn't know what else to say to someone like you," Heather said honestly.

"Something like 'Hi, I like your face', would have been safer, babe."

"Oh," Heather said, grinning, "now you tell me. But that day when you laughed," she said, her tone wistful, "I think I was hooked that moment."

Hunter chuckled. "Well, apparently you did something right, you got me to have dinner with you."

"Oh and that was the night I fell head over heels in love with you," Heather said.

"It is?" Hunter asked, surprised.

"When you looked at my painting and you understood it, you felt it," she said, putting her hand to Hunter's heart. "I knew you were meant for me then."

Hunter smiled, feeling tears well up in her throat. "I think I knew it then too, but I was completely freaked out by it."

"I know," Heather said, "that's why you kept running away."

"And you came after me," Hunter said, smiling, the tears in her eyes shining.

"Yes, I did," Heather said. "But when I found out I was pregnant with Sam, I really thought I'd lose you, I'd already started thinking I was losing you, but that just seemed to seal my fate. And then you got hurt."

"Yeah," Hunter said, nodding, "and when I woke up with you next to me in the hospital I knew that I loved you. I just needed to chew on it a bit, but I knew I didn't want to lose you."

Heather nodded. "I was so surprised when you asked me to marry you, I really thought I was dreaming."

"You made my life, babe…" Hunter told her, tears sliding from her eyes. "But we really need to stop this craziness with the chemo…"

Heather's eyes widened, and she drew in a breath, her eyes searching Hunter's.

"I know you've been doing it for me and Sam, babe," Hunter said, "but it's making you so sick. I don't want you to suffer, I love you too much to watch you do that and I know that all this shit in your veins isn't what you want, it isn't who you are."

She was crying at this point, because she knew what she was saying, and she knew it meant she'd have less time with the woman she loved so much, but she also knew it was the right thing to do.

Heather was crying too, sobbing because she knew that Hunter was giving up time with her—she loved her enough to know what Heather would do if she didn't have to think of anyone but herself. Stopping chemo would mean that the cancer could go back to spreading and would likely kill her faster. That's when the fear took over. Heather began to cry in earnest, shaking terribly.

"Babe?" Hunter queried, even as she gathered Heather carefully into her arms. "What is it"? she asked, her lips against Heather's forehead.

Heather breathed heavily, trying to calm down. Fear kept overwhelming her, though, engulfing her like an ocean wave.

"Talk to me, honey, what are you thinking?" Hunter asked.

"I'm so scared, Hunter…" Heather breathed, crying raggedly.

Hunter hugged her wife to her, fighting back the desire to scream at that moment. Why was this happening? Why were they being put through this? Why couldn't she help her wife when her wife really needed her?

"Listen, baby, listen…" Hunter said, desperate to help Heather through this. She pulled back, looking down at Heather, her hand caressing Heather's cheek and reaching up to brush back wisps of hair. "What do your own beliefs say about death?" she asked softly. "That *it's not really the end, right? That it's just moving to another plane of existence, right?"*

Heather swallowed hard a few times, but nodded her head, already calming down.

"So that's what's going to happen here, babe…" Hunter said, forcing her tone to be calm, and forcing back the agony that her heart was in at that moment. "And I'm going to be right here with you through all of it…you won't be alone, I'll be right here holding you." Tears dropped from her eyes, but she remained calm. "There's nothing to be afraid of," she told her.

Heather took slow breaths, looking up at Hunter. Putting her hand to Hunter's cheek, Heather felt her heart both heavy and swollen with pride and love for this woman.

"I want to leave this world with you and Sam next to me," she said.

"Then that's exactly how it'll happen," Hunter said. "I love you so much, babe. I just want you to be at peace and I don't want you to hurt anymore."

"Okay," Heather said, nodding. "Okay."

***

"Are you going home tonight?" Kori asked Hunter.

They'd been working together for a month, and things were going surprisingly smooth. Hunter found that working for Kori was actually pretty easy. Kori knew her well enough to leave her alone to work on projects. Hunter worked better when she was able to have free rein with her time, so Kori made a point of keeping as many meetings off Hunter's plate as she could. After some initial shocks in the office, it was working out well.

Hunter had stunned most of the clerical staff by walking in the first morning still wearing her aviator sunglasses, faded jeans, combat boots, and her army bomber-style flight jacket. She carried a Rockstar energy drink and had a very definite unpleasant look on her face. She'd waved away the young woman who was supposed to be her assistant.

"I need, caffeine, music, and solitude until nine if you expect me to be human," she'd told the girl. "If you want to wake the bear before then, keep your arms and feet inside the car at all times..." She let her voice trail off ominously on those last words. With that she walked into her new office and kicked her door closed.

Kori had heard about the incident five minutes later, her assistant found it endlessly amusing. Kori had simply laughed, shaking her head. "Yeah, Hunter's not a morning person."

"Yeah, I'm going home tonight," Hunter said, smiling, "why?"

Kori looked hesitant.

"What is it?" Hunter asked.

"I was wondering if you'd mind me coming home with you this weekend," Kori said.

Hunter looked back at her, surprised, then canted her head. "Why?"

Kori sighed, shrugging. "I guess I just want to see your mom and Fort Bragg again...I haven't been there since I left, you know."

"I know," Hunter said, grinning. "Sure, you can come home with me."

"Do you think Mom would have any rooms left at the inn?" Kori said.

Hunter smiled at Kori calling her mother 'Mom' like in the old days.

"Probably not, it's getting to be her busy season."

Kori nodded. "Well, I'm sure one of the other hotels has room," she said. "Or I could get over to Mendocino."

"Or you could just stay at the house, Kor, we have like four rooms," Hunter said.

Kori bit her lip. "I didn't want to intrude."

Hunter smiled softly. "You aren't."

"Okay," Kori said, smiling back at her.

Four hours later they were at the airport where Hunter was renting a pad, and Kori was climbing into Hunter's helicopter. As Hunter ran the engines up and did her preflight, she handed Kori a headset with a mic on it. As she put on the headphones, she tested the mic out, looking over at Hunter.

"I've never flown with you," she said into the mic, smiling.

"Nope," Hunter replied, shaking her head. "I'll try to keep it steady for you," she said with a wink.

"Oh good," Kori said, rolling her eyes.

Five minutes later Hunter was lifting off and Kori felt elated at the sensation. She could see the rapture on her face. This was one of Hunter's major loves.

They banked left and headed west toward the ocean.

"Oh my God, it's so beautiful from up here," Kori said, in awe.

"Oh yeah," Hunter said, smiling.

They flew in silence for a bit, just enjoying the view. Hunter had music playing, even in the helicopter. Even so, she kept in touch with Air Traffic Control all the way up the coast.

"So can I ask how much something like this cost?" Kori queried.

"One point six," Hunter replied.

"Holy shit!" Kori exclaimed. "How the hell do you have that kind of money?"

Hunter grinned, anyone else would have thought it rude ask that kind of question. Not Kori.

"Well, I sold the cottage a while back, and made a fairly good chunk of money on it, since Fort Bragg's gotten so popular and I owned it outright."

"You what?" Kori asked, looking surprised. "I thought that was like a rental or something..."

"No," Hunter said, shaking her head. "I owned it, I inherited it."

"Oh," Kori said, surprised.

Hunter grinned. "My family's been in Fort Bragg since around eighteen sixty, and they've owned a lot of land there since that time. We've been selling it little by little, but there's a lot to go around."

Kori's look changed. "So your family is kind of rich?"

Hunter looked considering, then shrugged. "It's established," she said. "Rich sounds like snobs and stuff. That ain't us, you know that."

"I do know that," Kori said nodding, having met many of Hunter's family members. "How many places do you own at this point?"

"A few," Hunter said with a grin. "As it is I own the land Heather and I built our house on, and that's around six acres. My family helped me build the house and outbuildings and helped me pour the pad for this when I needed it. So we really don't owe anything for it. I can probably get an easy three for it."

Kori stared back at Hunter for a long moment, shaking her head slowly. "Wow, Hunter..." she said, her shock evident on her face.

Hunter simply chuckled.

They talked about other things then, and before long they were turning to the east and heading in over land.

"You're not on the beach anymore, huh?" Kori asked.

"No," Hunter said, grinning, "but it's a nice view."

That statement was backed up a moment later when Hunter brought the helicopter down onto the helipad. The view was straight down to the ocean and incredibly beautiful on that warm, early spring day.

"Wow..." Kori said.

"Yep," Hunter said, nodding, "exactly what we said when we stood here on the bare land."

"I can see why," Kori said. Her eyes shifted to the house, and she could see why Hunter didn't want to give that up either.

The house was wood construction, with raised walkways all around, under which were beautiful gardens and water features. It was obvious that an artist had planned each and every area. Kori had never seen anything as stunning.

As they walked the perimeter of the house, Kori looked down into ponds, noticing the large Koi fish swimming in them. It was very quiet and peaceful. Kori found herself watching the fish wind their way around the plants and footings for the paths.

"Heather would sit and watch them for hours," Hunter said, grinning. "I could never understand how someone could watch fish for that length of time."

"She was an artist—it probably soothed and opened her mind," Kori said, her tone wistful.

Hunter's look flickered. "That exactly what she said it did."

Kori's eyes widened, not even sure where that had come from. "Jesus, is she possessing people too?"

Hunter chuckled. "Maybe…"

"Great…" Kori said, with a grin.

They walked into the house and Kori was overwhelmed with the light. There were huge windows, two stories tall, that faced the ocean. They let a lot of natural light into the house. Kori immediately noticed the picture in the living room: it was brightly colored, with varied textures. She could almost feel the picture without even touching it.

"That's beautiful," Kori breathed, glancing over at Hunter.

She saw that Hunter was staring beatifically up at the picture.

"That's the first painting Heather ever showed me of hers," Hunter said, stepping forward and touching the signature at the bottom of the canvas. It read 'Heather McLaughlin.' "The minute she put it in one of the shops in Fort Bragg I bought it, she didn't even know until after we got married."

"You're right, she was a great artist," Kori said. "I didn't even know you liked stuff like this." She canted her head at Hunter.

Hunter shrugged. "I didn't really care about it one way or the other until I met her. She showed me different artists and how they created their work, it was interesting," Hunter said, smiling softly. She thought about what Heather had said about falling in love with Hunter because she got her painting. Suddenly Hunter felt the lump in her throat and she swallowed convulsively against it.

"I'm—" Hunter began, her voice coming out gravelly. She cleared her throat and then started again. "I'm going to go change," she said then, "go ahead and look around."

"Okay," Kori said, seeing the sheen of tears in Hunter's eyes and knowing that talking about Heather had upset her.

A half an hour later when Hunter hadn't come back, Kori started to get worried and walked up the stairs, looking around. She knew that Samantha wasn't home—Hunter told her that she was on some senior trip—so she felt comfortable enough to look in various rooms to try and locate Hunter. She found the master bedroom and saw that the door was open. Walking to the doorway she glanced inside, she didn't see Hunter.

"Hunter?" she queried.

There were a few moments of silence, and then she heard Hunter call, "In here, I'll be out in a second."

Inside the walk-in closet, Hunter wiped away her tears, and finished pulling off her boots. She walked out into the main part of the room still wearing her jeans, but with her dress shirt complete unbuttoned and untucked: exposing a nice amount of skin alongside her black sports bra.

"Oh," Kori said, averting her eyes, but not before seeing that Hunter still looked every bit as good as she had years before.

Hunter chuckled as she reached up pulling off her shirt and tossing it in the hamper.

"You've seen a lot more than this," Hunter said, grinning.

Kor grinned. "Well, yeah, but…" She trailed off, thinking, *But I was allowed to jump you then.*

Hunter caught the look that crossed Kori's face and grinned at it.

"Do I want to ask what you were just thinking?" Hunter queried.

Kori pressed her lips together, her green eyes sparkling mischievously. "Probably not."

Hunter canted her head, narrowing her eyes slightly.

"Tell me," she said.

Kori shook her head. "Uh-uh."

"Why?" Hunter asked.

"Because," Kori said, "it was bad."

"Bad how?" Hunter asked, moving to sit on the bed, bringing her knees up to her chest, and draping her arms over them, still wearing just jeans and the black sports bra.

"Could you please put on a shirt?" Kori asked, trying not to stare at Hunter.

"Why?" Hunter asked, her silver eyes widening with mischief.

"Hunter Desolé Briggs!" Kori exclaimed. "Put a damned shirt on!"

Hunter laughed, shaking her head. "Now I'm definitely not putting on a shirt, in fact these jeans are getting a little—"

"That's not funny, don't you dare!" Kori growled. "Unless you—" she started to say, but then clamped her mouth shut. "Jesus Christ, what is it about this place?"

Hunter glanced around her and grinned, then shrugged. "Got me."

Kori looked around the bedroom, doing anything to keep her eyes of Hunter who looked far too good sitting on that bed. She looked at the picture on the wall, realizing it was very obviously a wedding picture. Hunter looked handsome in a black tuxedo, and Heather looked incredibly beautiful.

"She was really gorgeous," Kori said, her tone reflecting awe, "and you looked so handsome and so very happy…"

Hunter nodded sadly.

"This place is really beautiful, Hunter, I can see why you don't want to sell it."

"Beautiful is relative," Hunter said with a sad smile. "I don't want to sell it because it's her."

Kori drew in a breath, nodding as she blew it out. "I can see the butterfly thing you were talking about," she said, her eyes on the stained glass one hanging from the fan. "That's so beautiful," she breathed.

"That was the last one she bought," Hunter said, smiling softly.

"You're still having a really rough time, aren't you?" Kori said, sitting on the end of the bed, looking at Hunter.

Hunter drew in a deep breath, blowing it out slowly as she nodded.

"It's been getting better," she said, "having different work to do helps. It's keeping my mind active, so I don't have time to dwell, you know? But the nights just really suck."

Kori nodded, trying to understand. She couldn't fathom actually losing someone she truly loved. She did however think about how she'd felt when she'd heard Hunter had been hurt twenty years ago, and the thought of losing her was so devastating she could barely breathe. Hunter had actually lost Heather; her pain was immeasurable to Kori.

As if she knew what Kori was thinking, Hunter said, "She died right here," touching the bed next to where she sat.

"Oh Hunter…" Kori said, her voice a sad exhalation.

Hunter nodded. "It was the way she wanted it," she said, swallowing convulsively, "she wanted to die with me and Sam with her."

"That must have been so hard for you," Kori said, tears in her eyes suddenly. Hunter saw them, and turned her head, rubbing her cheek on her shoulder.

"She tried chemo, even though she hated any kind of chemical in her body," Hunter said, her tone haunted, "she was trying to stay alive for us."

"She loved you," Kori said.

"Yeah," Hunter said, her tone far away.

"You said she wants you to sell the house," Kori said gently, wanting desperately to help Hunter through this.

"Yeah," Hunter said, nodding. "She told me she wanted me to before she…" she began, but couldn't say the actual word.

"But she sent you signs too, right?" Kori asked.

"Yeah," Hunter said nodding, "this realtor's flyer kept asserting itself."

Kori raised an eyebrow. "How does that work?"

Hunter caught her look and couldn't help but smile. "Well, it started out by dropping down on my head from a closet, then it kept tumbling out of the trash no matter how many times I tried to dispose of it."

Kori widened her eyes. "I'd say she wants you to sell the house, Hunter."

"Ya think maybe?" Hunter asked. "Lately she's been making things go wrong in the house."

"Like?" Kori asked.

"Oh, plumbing, electrical," Hunter said, narrowing her eyes and glancing upward. "Stuff she knows I hate to fix!"

Kori couldn't help but laugh at that. For whatever reason she completely believed that Heather Briggs was indeed a spirit and was very definitely making her wishes known to her wife.

"Let me ask this," Kori said, reaching out to touch Hunter's hand, making a point of not looking at her still bare midriff.

Hunter grinned, noting Kori's pointedly averted eyes; remotely it really pleased her that Kori still found her attractive, even after twenty years.

"Are you going to ask, or do I have to divine it from you?" Hunter asked when Kori didn't continue. "I may have a wife in spirit, but I'm no medium or mind reader, Kor."

"You know..." Kori began, letting her voice trail off ominously.

"I do, yeah," Hunter said, grinning.

"Being a smart ass is just second nature to you, isn't it?" Kori asked.

"I think you knew that a long time ago, Kor," Hunter said, her eyes sparkling, but thoroughly enjoying bantering with Kori again.

"Can we get back on topic?" Kori asked.

"I don't know, can you get your eyes off my body?" Hunter asked, waggling her eyebrows at her, feeling like she had years ago when she'd teased Kori constantly.

"I'm gonna put my hands on your body in a minute, and it's going to be around your neck!" Kori said, widening her green eyes at Hunter threateningly, even as she grinned.

"Aw, see? That sounded good—till you got to that murderous part," Hunter glowered.

Kori looked back at Hunter, really wanting to ask if she could take back the murderous part and just do the other, but she knew it wasn't something Hunter could handle at that point. She was afraid to push too hard for something she desperately wanted, only to make Hunter back completely up from her. She knew losing Hunter again was more than she could handle, so she was willing to wait as long as it took to see if Hunter could be interested in her again.

Hunter saw the thoughts cross Kori's face and she knew that Kori wanted more right now, but she was grateful that Kori wasn't pushing. Hunter knew that she needed to take things slow in this area, because she didn't know exactly what her heart would allow at this point. The last thing she wanted was to hurt Kori with her inability to handle an emotional entanglement. She'd obviously hurt her once with her inability to commit, she didn't want to do it again.

"Now," Kori began, "what I was going to ask you is whether you think that part of you feels selling this house would mean you're forgetting about her." She gentled her voice on the last part, not wanting to hurt Hunter with her words.

Hunter drew in a deep breath, her look pensive, then she nodded. "Yeah, that could be part of it," she said honestly.

"Hunter, I think she's proven to you that she's not going anywhere," Kori said, "but I think she knows that you're not moving forward with your life if you're living here." She grimaced. "My God, babe, you're sleeping in the bed she died in…I can't even begin to think how hard that is for you."

Hunter felt a slight flutter of her heart when Kori called her 'babe' like she had before. Then she shrugged. "Probably why I don't sleep much."

"That's dangerous, Hunter," Kori said, her tone sharper than she meant it to be, but she knew she needed to get through to her. "Samantha already lost one mother, she can't lose you too."

Hunter looked back at Kori for a long moment, canting her head slightly.

"Tell me about your kids," she said.

Kori smiled, and Hunter recognized that look that a mother gets when someone asks her about her children. Heather always got it too.

"Why do want to know about my kids?" Kori asked.

"Because they're part of you," Hunter said. "And I've missed a lot, apparently."

"Oh," Kori said, "well, what do you want to know?"

"What do you want to tell me?" Hunter asked. "Hell what are their names? A boy and a girl, right?"

"Right," Kori said, nodding slowly, her look hesitant suddenly.

"What?" Hunter asked, canting her head at Kori's reluctance.

Kori bit her lip, closing her eyes as she grimaced. Finally she blew her breath out.

"My daughter's name is Desa, my son's name is Hunter," she said as quickly as possible.

Hunter's mouth fell open, her look perplexed. "Desa? As in—"

"Desolé," Kori said.

"Kor...why?" Hunter asked, her silver eyes reflecting confusion.

Kori pressed her lips together, her eyes not meeting Hunter's as she shrugged.

"I guess some crazy way to hold onto something about you...or a wish that..." she began, but shook her head, biting her lip again.

Hunter watched her, her look pained. "A wish that they'd been ours?"

Kori's lips trembled as she looked away. "I know it's stupid."

Hunter moved to take Kori in her arms, gathering her close.

"God, Kor, I'm sorry..." Hunter said against Kori's forehead. "I had no idea you felt like that about me when you left."

"I know, I didn't tell you, I was scared." Kori said.

"Because of the way I was..." Hunter said, grimacing and shaking her head, and pulling back just enough to look down at her. "I'm so sorry, Kor."

Kori rested her head against Hunter's neck, letting herself breathe in her scent, which was still so amazing.

"God we're a fucking mess, aren't we?" Hunter said laughing sarcastically, as she hugged Kori to her again. "And they let us run Cal Fire?" she asked, her tone ironic.

Kori started laughing then, so did Hunter. It felt good to laugh. When they both had laughed themselves out, Hunter kept her arms around Kori, leaning back to look down at her.

"So besides having the most amazing names, what else about them is awesome?"

"They're both gorgeous," Kori said, smiling.

"Like their mother," Hunter added.

"You making a pass at me?" Kori said, grinning.

"You'll know when I'm making a pass at you," Hunter said, grinning. She sounded so much like her old self that Kori found herself sighing.

"There's the Hunter Briggs I used to know," Kori said with a smile.

Hunter chuckled. "So what do they do?" she asked.

"Well, Hunter is in the military."

Hunter gave her a sidelong look. "Which branch?"

"Army, of course," Kori said, grinning.

"Ooah," Hunter said.

Kori laughed softly. "Uh-huh."

"And what's he doing in the military?" Hunter asked.

Kori pressed her lips together. "Um, he's a pilot."

"Nice…" Hunter said, grinning. "What's he flying?"

"Helicopters, what else?" Kori asked with a wink.

Hunter chuckled, nodding her head. "And what about Desa? Is her name Desa, or…"

"Her name is Desolé, we call her Desa," Kori said.

"Okay," Hunter said, shaking her head, "it's a little weird hearing my middle name so much."

"Oh, with the way you are, I'm sure you still hear it a lot from Mom," Kori said, winking at her.

"Anyway!" Hunter said, "So what is Desa doing?"

"She's actually getting ready to transfer to UC Berkley," Kori said.

"Seriously?" Hunter asked.

"Yeah," Kori said, "she's not an artist though, she's a Poly-Sci major."

Hunter nodded. "So she's smart like her mother too."

"And understand politics," Kori said, winking up at Hunter.

"Which ought to be entertaining with Trump in office," Hunter said, rolling her eyes.

"Tell me about it!" Kori exclaimed.

"So how about we go into town for dinner, and then you can see Mom?" Hunter suggested.

"That sounds great!" Kori said, smiling.

An hour later they were sitting down to dinner in Piaci Pub and Pizzeria. Hunter was greeted by a number of people. A couple of them actually recognized Kori as well. One older man in particular.

"Still so beautiful!" he exclaimed, hugging Kori.

"How are you, James?" Kori asked, smiling at him, remembering him well.

"Good, good! It's so good to see you two together again," he said, smiling and patting Hunter on the shoulder. "Hunter here's had it pretty rough," he said sadly.

Kori looked over at Hunter and saw Hunter smile at him softly.

James left, and Kori noticed that Hunter ordered a shot of tequila. The girl handed it to her with a wink and an "It's on me."

Kori looked at Hunter. "Does every woman in this town still flirt with you?" she asked, grinning.

Hunter drank the shot, and chased it with a drink of her beer. "More now," she said, shrugging. "I just think they're trying to make me feel better."

"Oh sure, 'cause that's what we women do, flirt with lesbians to make them feel better," Kori said, rolling her eyes and shaking her head. "You used to have better instincts than that, Hunter Briggs."

"They've been beaten down by marriage," Hunter said, grinning.

"Did they at least lay off while you were married?" Kori asked.

Hunter laughed at that. "Well, I can tell you that they didn't at first, but Heather wasn't exactly a complete hippie when it came to sharing."

"Uh-oh..." Kori said, widening her eyes. "What happened?"

Hunter grinned, "Oh, Heather overheard one of them say something to me and I'm not kidding you when I say I had to literally carry her out of the place before she scratched the girl's eyes out."

Kori laughed. "I like her style, I can think of a few times when I swear I wanted to beat the crap out of one of those women..." Kori said, letting her voice trail off as she grinned evilly.

"Oh, I see, now the truth comes out," Hunter said, laughing.

"Oh, every time you disappeared at night, I wanted to go hunt down whatever little tourist tramp you'd gone to see and kick her ass."

Hunter's eyes widened. "Did you say every time?"

Kori pressed her lips together, looking up. "Yeah," she said, her voice small.

Hunter shook her head. "You could have said something, you know."

"Right, and risk you telling me to buzz off?" Kori said, shaking her head. "I don't think so."

Hunter gave her a narrowed look. "Did it ever occur to you that you were the one I came back to every time?" she asked, her head canted.

Kori stared back at her for a long moment, her mouth hanging open. "No, it didn't," she said simply, looking completely flabbergasted.

"I always came back to you, Kor," Hunter said, "you were the only women I slept with consistently. Everyone else was a passing thing."

Kori shook her head, unable to believe that it had never occurred to her that Hunter had been telling her she was important to her all along. It wasn't in a traditional way but, then again, their relationship had been far from traditional.

"I'm so dumb sometimes," Kori said simply.

"Yes, you are," Hunter said, grinning.

"Hey!" Kori exclaimed, laughing as she did.

Later that evening, they walked into the inn, and Maggie could have raised the roof with her scream of delight at seeing Kori again.

"Oh my god, you're still so beautiful!" Maggie exclaimed, looking at Hunter. "Isn't she still beautiful?"

Hunter leaned back on the couch, crossing her legs. Her ankle over her knee, her left arm stretched out along the back of the couch.

"Yeah, Mom, she's still beautiful," Hunter said, grinning. She wanted to add "And still married to Tom" but decided against it.

Kori moved to sit on the couch, next to Hunter. They sat and talked for the next hour, catching up. A couple of times, Maggie noted that when Kori would sit back against the back of the couch, Hunter's arm would drop to rest on her shoulders lightly.

"Oh, Hunter," Maggie said at one point, "that garbage disposal is leaking again, can you take a quick look at it?"

Hunter rolled her eyes. "Firefighter, Mom, not plumber…" she said, even as she stood up. "I'll go take a look."

"Thank you, honey," Maggie said, patting Hunter on the butt as she walked by.

"Yeah, yeah…" Hunter muttered as she walked away.

Kori watched Hunter walk out, a smile on her lips. When she looked back over at Maggie she saw the look Maggie was giving her.

"What?" Kori asked.

"It's good to see the two of you together again," Maggie said, her eyes soft.

Kori turned her head slightly. "We're not together like that, Mom…" she said, not wanting Maggie to get the wrong impression—or, God forbid, for her to say something to Hunter and upset her.

"Oh, I know, I know," Maggie said, waving her hand dismissively, "but it's obvious she still cares about you, and I haven't seen her smile this much in almost two years, honey."

Maggie and Kori both grinned, looking toward the kitchen where Hunter could be heard cussing at the garbage disposal.

"She's got her sense of humor back," Maggie said, "and that's been in this last month working with you, Kori." Maggie's look was pointed. "I've been so worried about her," she said, "she was so devastated when she lost Heather. I thought I was going to lose her next, I really did."

Kori grimaced. "It was that bad?"

Maggie drew in a deep breath, nodding. "She was with Heather when she died, and according to Samantha she just fell apart. When the paramedics got there, Hunter collapsed. It took days before she'd even string enough words together to make a sentence. She wouldn't eat, she wouldn't sleep, she just sat outside in the dead of winter, staring down at the ocean. I was sure she was trying to catch pneumonia—as it was she gave herself an ulcer and lost so much weight. The day we buried Heather, I really thought Hunter would just crawl into the coffin with her, if there'd been one."

"If there'd been one?" Kori asked, curious.

"Heather was cremated and her remains were put into a contraption that grows a tree. It's in that huge pot in the center of the house," Maggie said. "That was Heather's way, with nature and all."

"Hunter says she was a hippie," Kori said, smiling.

"Not to hear Heather tell it," Maggie said, chuckling softly. "She said she was a bohemian girl. I never could figure out the difference, but I adored that girl and she loved Hunter so much." She said the last few words with a misting of tears in her eyes.

Kori nodded, wondering if Hunter had told her mother about the butterfly or any of the happenings in the house. She asked Hunter about it later that night on their way back to the house.

"Did you tell Mom about Heather being back?" Kori asked.

Hunter smiled at that feeling again when Kori called her mother mom, like she had years before. It felt right and she liked it. She shook her head.

"No," she said, "I didn't want to worry her more."

"What do you mean?" Kori asked.

"I mean she's had me under constant suicide watch since I lost Heather," she said, her tone serious. "I didn't want her to think I was now hallucinating visions of my dead wife. She might have me locked up."

Kori could see Hunter's point. "She's worried about you, babe, that shouldn't surprise you."

Hunter smiled softly, looking over at Kori. "Do you realize how often you call me babe?"

Kori's eyes widened, and she bit her lip. "I'm sor—" she started to say, but Hunter's hand on hers stopped her.

"It's okay, Kor," Hunter said. "I just wondered if you realized how quickly you slipped back into life here." She indicated to Fort Bragg.

Kori smiled softly. "I don't think I did, no." She slid her hand over Hunter's that still rested on her other hand. "Mom told me how bad things got for you after. And that you gave yourself an ulcer. Do you still have it?" she asked, looking concerned.

Hunter's lips twitched, but she nodded. She liked that Kori was holding her hand.

"What are you doing for it?" Kori asked.

Hunter grinned. "I have some stuff I can take when it gets bad."

"And when is that usually?"

Hunter didn't answer, just squeezed Kori's hand that rested under hers.

"That is not an answer, Hunter Desolé Briggs," Kori said, her eyes narrowed.

Hunter chuckled softly. "My stomach hurts most of the time," she said. "When it's really bad, I take something."

"But you had beer, pizza, and tequila tonight. Isn't changing your diet part of treatment?" Kori asked.

"Not mine," Hunter said.

"And what kind of Mickey Mouse doctor do you have that didn't change your diet?" Kori asked hotly.

Hunter laughed out loud at that. "Well, I'm my own Mickey Mouse doctor, so…"

"You're a firefighter, Hunter, not a doctor."

"I'm a paramedic too, Kor," Hunter said.

"Since when?" Kori asked.

"Since you left and I had too much time on my hands," Hunter told her, and then she shrugged. "Came in handy when I delivered Samantha in our bed."

"You delivered Samantha at home?" Kori asked.

"Hipp-ie," Hunter said slowly with a grin.

"Oh my God! That was brave and a little bit crazy on both of your parts."

"She didn't want to be in a hospital, and I was certified, so…it was what she wanted."

Kori smiled, nodding. "And you did anything she wanted, didn't you?"

"If I had the power to do it, yeah," Hunter said nodding. "That's what you're supposed to do for your lady."

Kori smiled at the statement. "And that's one of the things I've always loved about you," she said, "that gallant streak a mile wide."

Hunter looked over at her, shrugging, "It's a butch thing."

"It's a really cool thing," Kori corrected.

Later that night, Kori and Hunter retired to their rooms. Two hours later, Kori still couldn't sleep. She finally got up and walked downstairs. She was walking through the house—once again looking around at how incredible it was—when she came across the pot that Maggie had been talking about. A little tree was growing out of it. She stopped, standing near the pot that was two feet tall. The tree inside it was barely big enough to poke out, its tiny green leaves shining in the moonlight from the window above.

"I guess I should introduce myself," Kori said, "I'm Kori, but I'm betting you already know that, don't you?" She smiled softly. "You should know that I really care about Hunter, and I'll do whatever I can to help her stick around for Samantha. You got a really good one there." Kori paused, her smile turning sad. "I'm glad she found you, I just wish she'd been able to keep you forever. I would have liked to have met you. Although, I think I would have been really jealous of you. I couldn't hold on to her, you see. You did, and it sounds like she really, really loved you, so you must have been an amazing person. I'm truly sorry that this happened to you two." She said the last with tears in her eyes.

To her shock, Kori felt a warmth next to her. She looked, half expecting to see Hunter standing there. Regardless, she felt movement, like the warmth was moving around her. Then there was the sensation of what felt like a warm hand touch the spot over her heart and linger there. Although nothing was visible at all, Kori had the feeling she was not alone. She wasn't afraid, because she knew it was Heather and she honestly believed that Heather would know that her feelings for Hunter were genuine. She was sure that's why Heather had just touched her heart.

"You're here, aren't you?" Kori whispered, looking around her and over at the tree. She smiled softly, feeling very special that Heather had seen her worthy of a visit. "She misses you every day, Heather. I know that you know she needs to sell this house. I'm hoping I'm doing the right thing by trying to convince her to do that. If that's not what you want, you need to let me know. I just want Hunter to be okay—I love her too."

Kori would have sworn on a stack of Bibles that she felt a head rest against her shoulder at that moment. She closed her eyes, a tear escaping and rolling down her cheek. Somehow, she could feel all of the light and love that Heather had been and it brought her to further tears.

"The world lost a lot when it lost you, Heather," she said softly, "please help me save Hunter, because I know you know how amazing she is too." Again, she felt the hand on her heart. She took that as a yes, and smiled.

Hunter couldn't sleep, her stomach was killing her, so she finally got up and went downstairs to the kitchen. She passed Heather's tree, saying "Hey honey" softly as she did quite often when she thought she was alone. She didn't see Kori sitting on the couch in the living room, or that Kori had looked up, watching her moving around in the kitchen.

"What's that?" Kori asked from the living room.

Hunter jumped, as she turned to look at Kori. Setting the glass in her hand down and putting both hands on the counter in front of her, she bent forward and did her best to slow her heart rate that had just leaped at the sound of Kori's voice.

"Jesus! Scare the shit out of me why don't you?" Hunter queried.

Kori chuckled. "I'm sorry. I guess I figured you were used to women appearing in your house randomly."

"Just my resident ghost," Hunter said, grinning as she picked up the glass and downed the contents.

"So what is that?" Kori asked again.

"For my stomach," Hunter said, rinsing the glass and putting it in the dishwasher.

"Bad?" Kori asked concern in her voice.

Hunter shrugged. "Bad enough to take something," she said simply as she walked into the living room, sitting down on the couch near Kori. "What are you doing up?"

"Couldn't sleep," Kori said, "so I came down here and got a visit from your wife."

"Uh-oh, what did she do?" Hunter asked, not sounding surprised by what Kori had said.

"Nothing bad," Kori said. "Mostly it felt like she wrapped her arms around me and put her hand on my heart. It felt like she put her head on my shoulder, too, and I swear Hunter, I could feel everything she was in that moment…" She shook her head as her voice trailed off in wonder. "She was really amazing, wasn't she?"

Hunter drew in a deep breath, nodding as she blew the breath out. "Yeah, yeah she was."

They talked for the next hour and Hunter told Kori more about Heather. After a while, it became evident that Hunter was getting tired, and Kori felt her eyes drooping as well.

Hunter stood up. "Come on," she said, holding her hand out to Kori.

"Where are we going?" Kori asked as she took Hunter's hand.

"Back to bed," Hunter said simply. With that she turned and led Kori back toward the stairs. As she passed Heather's tree, Hunter said, "Quit harassing people," with a grin. The next step she stumbled slightly. "And I'd swear I just got pushed…" she said, still grinning.

Kori laughed. "I guess you'd better be nice then."

"Uh-huh," Hunter murmured as she continued past the master and led Kori to the guest bedroom she was staying in.

"Um?" Kori queried as Hunter opened the door for her.

"It's obvious neither of us can sleep alone, let's give this a try."

"Now I'm the one that's gonna get pushed," Kori muttered under her breath as she moved to lay down on the bed, "probably out a window…"

Hunter laughed, shaking her head as she climbed into the bed next to Kori. "No, she knows about you and was actually wanting me to contact you before."

"Really?" Kori asked as she shifted to make room for Hunter on the bed.

"Yep," Hunter said nodding. "She considered you unfinished business for me."

"Wow…" Kori said. "I wouldn't have wanted anyone like me that close to you."

"Like you?" Hunter asked, turning on her side and looking at Kori.

"Yeah, you know with our past and all," Kori said. "I'd be afraid to lose you."

"Oh she was back in the early days," Hunter said, "but near the end, she just wanted me to be happy and she thought you'd do that for me."

Kori pressed her lips together, blinking a couple of times, then blew her breath out. "She really loved you. I could feel that tonight, it was so prevalent and wrapped up in her…I don't know how to explain it."

Hunter hugged Kori to her, putting her chin on the top of Kori's head. "I know she loved me, I never doubted that. I doubted that I was capable of moving on from her. I still don't know, Kor, you know? That's why I'm holding back with you," she said, pulling back to look down at Kori. "I don't want to hurt you again."

Kori reached her hand up between them, touching Hunter's face.

"And I'm willing to wait for you to be sure," Kori told her, "but I want to be here for you now, if you'll let me."

Hunter grinned, looking down at their bodies close together. "This is me letting you, Kor."

"Good," Kori said, smiling.

They fell asleep laying as they were, and they both slept deeply for the first time in a long while.

***

They'd stopped chemotherapy and withstood the warnings that Heather's health would deteriorate drastically with this course of action.

"We're done," Hunter had told the doctor. "That's all you need to know."

With that, she'd hung up the phone. The whole family had been told what they were doing, so they visited off and on for days on end— sitting and talking to Heather, sharing stories and sometimes just sitting silently with her. Hunter sat by, watching her family and her wife, and felt constantly blessed by the amazing people she was related to. Members of the town, as well as Hunter's Cal Fire family came by too. More than once Hunter had to threaten to throw one of her colleagues out for trying to tell one too many stories about Hunter Briggs and her antics. Family members also brought food and drink, telling Hunter constantly that she was too thin. They were surrounded by love in those last few weeks.

Every night, Hunter fell asleep holding Heather in her arms as gently as she could. For a week or so, Heather actually rallied. Hunter took her shopping during that time, and she bought another butterfly. It took Hunter everything she had to keep from bursting into tears, because she knew it was likely the last one Heather would ever buy.

One morning, Hunter woke to the feel of Heather's fingers on her face. She opened her eyes, looking down at her wife. Heather's blue eyes were sunken and faded, and Hunter knew that cancer was taking everything away from her at this point.

"Hey there, beautiful," Hunter said softly, "what's going on?"

Heather was breathing heavily, and Hunter could see she was in pain.

"You're hurting," Hunter said. "Do you want a shot?" she asked, praying Heather would say yes. To her surprised, Heather nodded. "Okay baby, hold on," Hunter said, reaching for the med pen they'd prescribed for Heather for managing her pain. "What we talking, hon? Three? Four?"

"Five," Heather uttered in a soft gasp.

"Oh babe..." Hunter said, her voice sorrowful. "Okay, I got you," she said, using the pen to give Heather the injection, then setting it aside and rubbing the spot gently. "You should feel it soon, okay?" Hunter said, her tone soothing. "There it goes," she said, seeing Heather start to relax.

"Hunter, I love you so much..." Heather said softly, her eyes staring up at her.

"I love you, honey," Hunter said, smiling. "Is the pain better?"

Heather nodded. "I'm so tired..." she said then, her voice breathless as she closed her eyes for a second.

Hunter knew at that moment that she was about to lose her wife. The pain of it tore through her. She pressed her lips together, lifting her head so Heather couldn't see her face, knowing that it would only make Heather feel worse. Hunter's insides were quaking, feeling like everything inside her was turning to jelly.

"Rest honey," Hunter said, trying to keep her voice normal.

Heather was shaking her head. "I wanted to grow old with you..." she said, breaking Hunter's heart a little bit more.

"I wanted that too, baby…" Hunter said, tears sliding down her cheeks at that point, she couldn't stop them. "But it seems that you're needed elsewhere."

"I don't want to go," Heather said, tears falling from her eyes.

"I know, honey," Hunter said, "I know, but it's okay to go."

"Where's Sam?" Heather asked suddenly.

"Samantha!" Hunter yelled, not wanting to leave Heather for even a moment.

Samantha responded instantly to the tone of Hunter's voice and came running into the room. Hunter looked at her, tears in her eyes, and Samantha knew that her mother was dying. To her credit, Samantha drew in a deep breath and walked over to the bed, laying down behind Heather.

"I'm here, Mom, right here," Samantha said, as she kissed Heather's cheek.

"Samantha, you take care of your mother, okay?" Heather told her daughter.

Samantha pressed her lips together, tears forming in her eyes. as she nodded. "I will."

"I love you, honey…" Heather said to Samantha. "Make sure you go to college and marry someone nice…"

Samantha was crying outright then, nodding even as she tried not to beg her mother to stay. She and Hunter had talked about it, and Hunter had explained that they needed to tell Heather that it was okay to go if it was time. Samantha knew this was that time.

"I love you, Mom," she said. "I promise, college and the best person on the planet for marriage…only if Mom says the person meets her approval."

"Oh don't wait for that, you'll never get married," Heather said, smiling weakly.

They smiled back, even as tears fell.

Heather looked at Hunter again, raising a shaking hand to touch Hunter's face.

"I love you so much," Heather said, taking Hunter's hand. "Please take care of yourself, Hunter, please…I can't go thinking that you won't be okay."

"I'll be okay, honey," Hunter told her, knowing she was lying, but hoping Heather believed it. "We'll be okay. It's okay to let go, honey…it's okay," Hunter said, hugging Heather to her, gritting her teeth as the agony of the moment tore at her. Leaning down, she kissed Heather's lips tenderly. She felt Heather kiss her back and squeeze her hand gently. Then she was gone.

Hunter let out a sob, and hugged Heather to her, finally able to cry and rage and make all the noise she wanted to. Sobs racked through her as she shook and held Heather's body against her. Samantha cried harder knowing that her mother was gone, watching her other mother fall completely apart.

"I can't, I can't…" Hunter said, gasping and crying at the same time. "I can't do this…I can't…Sam…I can't…" She shook her head, breathing heavy and fast. "I can't pronounce…not her…not my Heather…oh God…" she moaned, as a fresh wave of pain slammed into her. "Call the paramedic have them bring…the coroner," Hunter said, choking on the last word.

"Okay, okay," Samantha said, willing to do anything to keep from losing Hunter too.

When the paramedics arrived with the coroner, Hunter had to be almost forcibly removed from Heather. As soon as Hunter moved to stand, she collapsed, hitting the floor with terrifying force.

***

Hunter had made the decision to sell the house. She, Kori, Samantha, and an army of Hunter's family set to clearing away all her belongings to put it on the market. There were a few tenuous moments when Hunter had to leave a room because she was having a hard time. One such time she walked outside and to the edge of the property, looking down at the ocean, tears in her eyes. As she stood staring at the water, she felt a warmth behind her, and what felt like a head on her shoulder. She closed her eyes, nodding her head. She knew it was Heather's spirit; she'd felt it the whole weekend near her, encouraging her. Kori had commented on it the night before as they lay on the bed in the guest bedroom. Hunter had told Kori that she didn't feel right bringing any other woman into the bed she'd shared with Heather. "I remember how pissed you got at me for letting another woman into the bed you shared with me…Heather was like you in that respect."

Kori had agreed whole heartedly.

The night before, Kori had said, "She's been here a lot, hasn't she?"

Hunter nodded. "It feels like it, yeah."

"She knows this is hard for you," Kori had said.

"Yeah," Hunter had breathed.

Kori had tightened her hold on Hunter then, and Hunter had let Kori soothe her to sleep, stroking her hair the way Hunter had always loved.

Now, staring out at the ocean, Hunter drew in a couple of deep breaths, feeling Heather ease away from her as Kori walked up.

"You okay?" Kori asked softly, walking up and doing basically what Hunter had felt Heather had been trying to do, sliding her arms around Hunter's waist from behind, resting her head against Hunter's back.

Hunter covered Kori's hands with hers. "Yeah," she said softly, "I just got overwhelmed for a second."

"Do we need to stop?" Kori asked.

"No," Hunter said, shaking her head, "I need to get through this and get the house sold, before Heather wreaks more havoc."

The hot water heater had gone out two days before, even though it was only two years old. Hunter got a warranty replacement but had cussed a blue streak the whole time as she installed it. "You know I hate plumbing, Heather, why do you keep messing with it?" Kori had heard her ask. She also heard her answer herself: "Because you know I hate plumbing. I know, I know, sell the damned house, Hunter. I'm trying! Stop breaking shit!"

Kori had chuckled to herself and purposely kept family members away from the garage at that point.

To everyone's surprise the house sold in two days, and Hunter received multiple offers with a bidding war eventually developing. She ended up with an insane amount of money from it, but the new owners wanted a short escrow of two weeks. Fortunately a lot of packing had been accomplished in the first round, so the second round was easier and faster.

The morning dawned when they were set to move. Hunter had found an apartment in the city in the Castro. She was set to move in early there as well—Samantha was moving into the dorms at UC Berkley.

Kori got up early and went down to make coffee. Samantha came running downstairs calling for Kori, her voice terrified.

"Kori, come quick! Mom's losing it…it's like when Mom died!"

Kori ran up the stairs with Samantha hot on her heels. Kori was shocked by what she saw. Hunter was curled up on the bed in almost a fetal position, crying and shaking her head, saying, "I can't, I can't…"

Walking over to the bed, Kori sat down, glancing over at Samantha who stood in the doorway, wringing her hands nervously.

"Hunter?" Kori said, reaching out to touch her shoulder.

Hunter was breathing heavily, tears streaming from her eyes. "I can't do this Kor…" she said, her voice ragged.

Kori lay down behind Hunter, wrapping her body around hers and reaching up to stroke her hair.

"Babe, we talked about this…Heather's not just this house, she's always going to be with you," she said, her tone soothing. "We've got the guys coming that are going to take extra care with her getting her to the new apartment, everything's fine…"

Hunter shook her head again. "I can't…" she said again, her voice choking up. "We need to cancel the sale, I'll pay whatever I have to, I can't leave…I can't…"

"Hunter…" Kori began.

"No!" Hunter yelled, scaring both Kori and Samantha with both the volume and the vehemence with which she said it.

Kori winced, but continued to hold Hunter. "Okay, so maybe we wait a little longer..." she began, thinking maybe things were moving too fast.

"Kori..." Samantha said.

Kori looked up and saw that Samantha was looking toward the window. Kori looked over and saw the butterfly.

"Hunter, she's here," Kori said softly.

Hunter slowly sat up and watched as the butterfly fluttered around the room, landing on boxes and pieces of furniture. Then it flew over to Hunter, landing on her shoulder. She closed her eyes slowly, her lips trembling.

"I can't do it babe..." Hunter said, her voice tremulous. "I can't..."

She opened her eyes and looked over at the butterfly, watching as it flapped its wings slowly. She swore she could see Heather's eyes narrowing at her—somehow she could feel the warning in this simple insect's look. Hunter heard glass break somewhere in the house.

"Seriously?" she asked the butterfly. "You're threatening me now?"

Kori and Samantha exchanged grins. To anyone else this would seem insane. The butterfly's wings continued to flap and Hunter felt a push at her shoulder, from the opposite side where Kori sat.

"Butterflies are supposed to be peaceful, Heather," Hunter said. "Aren't you breaking some hippie code?" she asked with a grin.

Again she could swear she could feel Heather's annoyance. More glass broke.

"What are you destroying down there? I hope it's those glasses your agent bought us, you know I hated those things…" She glanced at Kori. "They were stupid heavy ass things, more like paperweights than beer mugs. The woman was clueless about beer."

The butterfly flew up and hovered near Hunter's lips, its antennae brushing her lips.

"Okay, that tickles," Hunter said, grinning.

"I think that was a kiss," Samantha said as she walked toward the bed, canting her head. "Hi Mom."

The butterfly floated over to Samantha, repeating the gesture with her.

"I love you too," Samantha said, tears misting her eyes. "I miss you. I'm going to Berkley, did you hear? I'm going to study art, like you wanted me to."

The butterfly flew around in an intricate pattern.

"That looks like pride," Kori said, grinning.

Samantha smiled, tears sliding down her cheeks.

The butterfly made its way to Kori then, and Kori stayed still as it hovered in front of her face. Kori felt the warmth on her heart again.

"I'll take care of them, I promise," Kori said softly. "Don't be a stranger."

With that the butterfly moved to Hunter again for a moment, then flew back toward the window and out. There was a ring at the door.

"Sounds like the movers are here," Kori said, looking at Hunter, "what do you say?"

Hunter drew in a deep breath, then nodded slowly. "I say, let's do this."

Later that night, Hunter flopped down on her brand new bed. Kori lay down sideways on the bed, looking up at Hunter.

"We're getting too old for this moving shit," Hunter complained.

"Speak for yourself, I'm only forty!" Kori said, grinning.

"I was speaking for myself, but you look tired too," Hunter said.

"I'm exhausted!" Kori said.

Hunter looked over at her for a long moment. "Are you going home tonight?"

Kori looked pensive. "I hadn't really thought about it yet, why?"

Hunter shrugged, "Well, I figure he expects you home since you're now here in the city and not up in Fort Bragg helping me."

Kori nodded. "Yeah, I'm sure he expects me home tonight."

"Kor, why do you stay with him if you don't love him?" Hunter asked, moving so she was lying face to face with Kori.

"Why leave him so I can be alone, Hunter?" Kori countered.

Hunter blew her breath out. "I want you to be happy, Kor…you deserve to be happy."

"Besides my kids, you were the only one that made me happy," Kori said.

Hunter stared back at her for a long moment, then, to Kori's shock, moved to kiss her lips softly. "Then leave him and be with me."

Kori stared back at Hunter for a long few moments, her mind telling her that there's no way she'd just heard what Hunter had said correctly. Had she meant that? Or was she just in the moment?

"Do you mean that?" Kori asked, her eyes searching Hunter's.

"Babe, I don't say things I don't mean," Hunter said, "you know that."

Kori smiled softly. "I love you, I never stopped loving you…"

Hunter leaned in to kiss her lips again. "Show me," she whispered against Kori's lips.

Kori moved to push Hunter onto her back, her lips going to Hunter's neck, kissing and moving up to her ear. "I love you…" she whispered again, she moved down Hunter's body, kissing her.

Before long, Hunter pulled her up and put her under her, then it was Hunter's turn to take her time. Moving down Kori's body and making her writhe, Kori's hands grasped at Hunter. Hunter took her time, making Kori tremble with her need for release. Even then, Hunter continued to kiss and caress her, removing each piece of clothing, slowly. Her fingertips brushed past hard and aching nipples, making Kori gasp and shudder. When Kori lay completely naked, Hunter started at her feet, kissing, touching, and caressing. Kori moaned, her hips bucking, wanting Hunter so much she could barely stand it. Still Hunter took her time, savoring every inch of Kori's skin. When she lay between Kori's parted legs, she used her tongue slowly and so gently that Kori was begging her for release. Then, without warning, Hunter slid her body up Kori's, pressing her hips against hers in a grinding motion. Kori was coming instantly and Hunter wasn't far behind.

They spent the next few hours rediscovering each other and driving each other completely insane, enjoying every second of it.

When they lay afterwards, their bodies still intimately intertwined, Hunter moved her lips to Kori's ear.

"Thank you for helping me through all of this," she whispered, "and for giving me the time I needed to be sure about this." She kissed Kori's temple, bringing her hand up touch her cheek as she pulled back to look into Kori's eyes. "I love you, Kor."

Kori smiled, her eyes lighting up as she did. "You don't know how long I've waited to hear you say that to me."

"Well, the wait is over," Hunter said, grinning.

"So," Kori said, sliding her hand over Hunter's arm slowly, "I gotta say, you've really got that controlled burn down…" Her voice trailed off seductively.

Hunter leaned in, kissing Kori's lips again and reigniting the fire between them. As she moved over her, she said, "Expert level, baby, expert level."

Epilogue

Long legs clad in skinny jeans; a burgundy silk top clinging to curves that wet dreams were made of; bright green eyes that picked up the sparkle from the eyeshadow she wore; long sweeping lashes; extremely kissable lips. A tumble of rich, dark red hair, and just enough jewelry to catch the light and cause the diamonds at her ears to wink and shine. Everything looked good, and then there were the black combat boots with a heel. Seriously? It was all Dax needed to see, and she was done.

At the table, Kori looked over at Hunter, seeing that she was watching Dax with a grin on her lips.

"Think we should tell her?" Kori asked Hunter.

Hunter's grin widened. "Nah, let's just see what happens."

Kori shook her head, blowing her breath out as she put her chin down on Hunter's shoulder and watched the scene unfold.

Dax Ray walked up to the bar, summarily dismissing the redhead for a complete lack of respect to military personnel everywhere. She put her tattooed hand on the bar, the tattoo of a jet and the words 'Fighter Weapons School' and 'Top Gun' with two hash marks at the top on her right forearm also on display as the shirt sleeves of her denim work shirt were rolled up to expose all of her tattoos.

"Hey, Tam, gimme a beer," Dax said to the bartender.

"You got it, Dax," Tammy replied, smiling.

The redhead looked over at her, looking at her arm.

"Pilot, huh?" the girl asked.

Dax barely spared her a glance of disdain. "Yeah," she answered simply.

"Navy?" the girl asked then.

"Uh-huh," Dax replied, her lips curled in obvious condescension.

"So a navy pilot, that was a top gun?" the girl clarified.

Dax lost her patience. "Yeah, honey, and where I come from," she said, glancing down at the girl's footwear with disgust, "we don't wear combat boots as a fashion accessory."

To Dax's surprise, rather than shrinking from her derision, the girl turned to face her.

"I take it you were deployed," the woman said, her green eyes sparkling in amusement now, amusement that Dax didn't understand at all.

"Yeah, I did three tours in Iraq, what's your point?" Dax practically snapped.

"And that," the woman said, circling her finger at Dax to indicate her whole person, "is the attitude you brought back with you?"

"Yeah, take it or leave it, babe," Dax practically growled.

The girl canted her head slightly, her green eyes almost wicked now, as she made a sucking sound through her teeth. "Too bad," she said, "you were kind of cute."

With that the redhead walked away, her friend trailing after her. Dax turned to watch her go and couldn't deny that the movement on the girl's hips had a hell of a nice swing to them. She smacked herself in the forehead, shaking her head as she did.

"Dax!" the bartender called to get her attention, handing Dax her beer.

Dax continued to watch as the redhead made her way to the dance floor. The song on had a seductive edge—it was The Veronica's 'Take Me On the Floor' and the verse of the song had a very sexy slant to it.

Dax didn't want to watch the girl dance, but it was hard not to: she had some seriously seductive moves that were rather distracting. Again, Dax reminded herself that the woman was obviously a twit. Picking up her beer, she walked back to the table where Hunter and Kori sat with two other couples. Dax liked the new chief deputy director—Hunter knew her stuff when it came to aviation.

Sitting down at the table, Dax turned her ball cap around backwards, taking a long swig of her beer. Hunter looked over at her.

"So what was that?" Hunter asked, nodding toward the redhead on the dance floor.

Dax shrugged. "She annoyed me."

Hunter licked her lips looking amused. "Yeah?"

"She's wearing combat boots with a heel, why can't the girls just stick with stilettos without going after the military look? No offense, Director," she added, looking at Kori.

Kori crossed her legs, her stilettos fully on display. "No problem," she said with an odd smile on her lips.

"Yeah…" Hunter said, her look sardonic. "I guess I should tell you…"

"Tell me what?" Dax asked.

"That," Hunter said, pointing to the redhead, "is your new boss."

About the Author

Sherryl D Hancock is from California is the bestselling author of the lesbian romance *WeHo* series. Her books regularly touch on important topical issues such as mental health, the Don't Ask, Don't Tell policy and abuse.

You can find more on the author and her books at: sherrylhancock.com and vulpine-press.com

Also by Sherryl D. Hancock:

The lesfic *WeHo* series follows a group of women from Los Angeles as they navigate the ups and downs of love, life, work, and everything in between.

www.vulpine-press.com/we-ho

The *MidKnight Blue* series. Dive into the world of Midnight Chevalier and as we follow her transformation from gang leader to cop from the very beginning.

www.vulpine-press.com/midknight-blue-series

The *Wild Irish Silence* series. Escape into the world of BJ Sparks and discover how he went from the small-town boy to the world-famous rock star.

www.vulpine-press.com/wild-irish-silence-series

CPSIA information can be obtained
at www.ICGtesting.com
Printed in the USA
BVHW030355110821
614083BV00024B/178